THE RUNT

Since Robert Purdy's family perished in a fire two years back, the youth has had to survive as best he can in New York, dodging the police and street gangs alike. When he trespasses on one gang's patch and they exact their revenge by stabbing his friend, Robert jumps on a train and ends up in Rock Springs, Wyoming Territory. Can this city boy learn the life of a cowpoke, how to handle six-guns and steers — and eventually face off against rustlers?

Books by Billy Hall
in the Linford Western Library:

KID HAILER
CLEAR CREEK JUSTICE
THE TEN SLEEP MURDERS
KING CANYON HIDEOUT
MONTANA RESCUE
CAMBDEN'S CROSSING
WHEN JUSTICE STRIKES
THE TROUBLE WITH THE LAW
SANDHILLS SHOWDOWN
KID PATTERSON
COWARD'S CARNAGE
CASTOFF COWHAND
EAGLE'S PREY
HARD AS NAILS
TEMPTATION TRAIL
DAKOTA DEATH
RUSTLER'S RANGE
IN NEED OF HANGING
SOFT SOAP FOR A HARD CASE
RANGE OF TERROR
DUEL OF SHADOWS
BULL'S EYE STAGE COACH
THE BRONC BUSTER
SAM AND THE SHERIFF
BLIND-SIDED
THE BOUNTY HUNTER

BILLY HALL

THE RUNT

Complete and Unabridged

LINFORD
Leicester

First published in Great Britain in 2014 by
Robert Hale Limited
London

First Linford Edition
published 2017
by arrangement with
Robert Hale
an imprint of The Crowood Press
Wiltshire

A catalogue record for this book is available
from the British Library.

ISBN 978–1–4448–3200–6

Published by
F. A. Thorpe (Publishing)
Anstey, Leicestershire

Set by Words & Graphics Ltd.
Anstey, Leicestershire
Printed and bound in Great Britain by
T. J. International Ltd., Padstow, Cornwall

This book is printed on acid-free paper

1

Robert Purdy hunched down deeper into the over-sized coat. His cap was pulled low over his eyes. From beneath its leather bill he watched the people who crowded the sidewalk.

Though it was dusk, light streamed from the store windows. The street lamp lighters were making their rounds, lighting the gas lamps along the street. It was perfect. There was light enough to see a good mark. The shadows were deep enough they would never see his face.

A portly gentleman stopped in front of one of the stores. He smiled as he looked at the display of toys in the window.

'Perfect!' Robert breathed.

He pulled the oversized coat up a little higher around his ears and his muscular shoulders forward to hide their bulk. He was scarcely 5' 5", so it was easy, in the oversized clothes, to appear much younger than his eighteen years.

He approached the rotund gentleman. He spoke in a high-pitched voice, with just a hint of whine. The voice pictured a torrent of tears held back by firm resolve.

'Please, mister? Could y'spare a few cents? Just a few pennies, maybe?'

The man frowned with irritation. Then he noticed the rags wrapped around the boy's feet for warmth against the December chill. He hesitated.

'My ma's bad sick, mister. I gotta get 'er somethin' t'eat. Just two bits'd let 'er eat a real meal.'

Sighing, the man reached inside his jacket. Pulling a fat wallet from an inner pocket, he opened it. Squinting in the dim light, he peered inside, trying to be sure of the number on the bill. It was obvious he was feeling very generous, going for the wallet instead of his coin purse.

Too quickly for the overweight man to react, Robert propelled into him, plunging a rock-solid shoulder into the soft midsection of the surprised gentleman.

At the same time he grabbed the wallet, wresting it from the man's hand with an iron grip.

The man gasped as the wind was driven from him. He plumped down on the sidewalk, stunned again by the force of his bulk landing on the unyielding surface. He fell backward on to his back, trying desperately to force air into his lungs.

A passerby rushed to him. 'You OK, mister?'

The gentleman opened and closed his mouth like a fish in the air. No sound came forth.

'You OK?' the man asked again. A crowd began to gather. 'You took quite a spill, there. Here, raise your arms like this.'

He raised the man's arms above his head, trying to help him pump air into his lungs. After a couple of minutes, the obese gentleman was able to suck air into his lungs.

'Robbed,' he wheezed.

'What? What did you say?'

He gasped another breath into his lungs. 'Robbed,' he wheezed. 'Police! Get the police! That kid took my wallet.'

The man who had come to his aid looked around. The only people in sight were the crowd that had gathered. A policeman shouldered his way through.

'Here, here! What's goin' on?' he demanded.

'The man says he was robbed,' someone explained.

'That so?' the policeman demanded.

'He was a little kid!' the gentleman said. His color was beginning to return to normal. 'He asked for a handout. I took out my wallet, and he knocked me flat. Took the whole wallet! Go get him!'

The policeman shook his head. 'No chance o' catchin' him,' he said. 'Sounds like one o' the gangs. They look like kids, some of 'em. Tougher'n sailors, they are. Lucky he knocked you down instead o' stickin' you. Here, I'll help you up.'

He placed his hands under the gentleman's arms and lifted. A couple other men rushed to help. Together they helped the man lift his bulk from the sidewalk. 'You OK, then?' the policeman asked. 'Nothin' broken?'

The gentleman took a deep breath. 'Only my pride, and a goodly sum of money, I'm afraid.'

'Did you get a good look at 'im?'

He shook his head. 'Didn't see his face at all. Coat was way too big on him. His shoes, or his feet, couldn't tell which, were wrapped in rags.'

'Well, he's long gone by now,' the policeman commiserated.

And he was. By that time Robert was three blocks away, furtively making his way to his hideout. As soon as he barreled into the gentleman and grabbed the wallet, he ducked down an alley. Running full speed, he went through the alley, turned along the next street, then ducked into a crowd of people making their way along the sidewalk. He clung tightly to the wallet, keeping it out of sight inside his coat.

Three blocks down the street he darted down another alley, then ducked into the darkness of a doorway. He stood there, invisible in the deepening shadows, watching. There was no indication he had been followed. Nothing betrayed that anyone had noticed him at all.

He waited for a full hour, scarcely moving. The sidewalks emptied. Staying against the building, he moved quietly to the end of the block. He crossed the street, watching carefully all around. He passed by a burned-out building. One corner of the building still jutted skyward. The smell of old smoke clung heavily in the air.

At the still-standing corner of the building, he stopped again. He listened carefully. After a long wait, he said softly, 'Ya in there, Pat?'

From the burned out ruins a voice responded, 'Yeah. You get somethin'?'

Darting a look around again, Robert stepped around the corner. He dropped to his knees and backed into a small window well. He slithered through the window into a corner of the basement of the burned out hulk. When it had caved in, the collapsing timbers had bridged across this spot, leaving a space the size of a large room. Neither of them knew how precariously the charred timbers protected their hidden corner. They only knew it provided a perfect shelter against the cold, against their enemies, and against the ever-present threat of discovery by the police.

Robert lifted a flat section of some former wall and covered the window. He felt all around it, being sure that it was perfectly in place so that no sliver of light could escape. Then he hung a blanket on nails above the window, so it covered it yet again.

'You can light the lamp now,' he said.

A match flared, then the wick of a kerosene lamp came to life. Pat shook the match out and put the chimney back on the lamp. A dim, yellowish light flooded the compartment.

In the flickering light, Robert could see both beds, made with a collection of old blankets scavenged from who knows where. There was little else in the compartment, except the lamp, sitting on the floor.

Robert sat down on the floor and leaned against the wall. 'Got a good one, I think.'

Pat sat down cross-legged to watch, as Robert hauled out the wallet. He whistled softly as Robert opened it. 'Wow! Who ever carries that kind o' money around with 'im? How much is there?'

Robert swallowed hard. 'It looks like more'n a hundred dollars!'

'I ain't never seen a hundred dollars!'

'Me neither. My pa had a twenty dollar bill once. In fact, that was the day of the fire. He'd just got paid. Brought home a whole bunch of groceries, and a new pair of shoes for Rance, an' a doll for Coleen, an' a pocket knife for me.'

'Like Christmas,' Pat marveled.

'Yeah,' Robert agreed. 'Till the fire.'

'You're lucky you got out.'

'I almost didn't. Shinnied down that drain pipe, when I couldn't get to any of the rest of them.'

'Lucky it didn't just bust off.'

A soft sound from outside interrupted

their conversation. Pat swiftly blew the lamp out. They held their breath.

A voice drifted through the boarded up window. 'You sure he went in here?'

'Positive,' a second voice replied. 'I followed him almost to here before, so I hid out over there in that yard and waited. I seen 'im slippin' along, then he ducked into that window. There must be a space that ain't full o' caved-in stuff.'

'OK. Get ready then,' the first voice advised. 'All of you. He's tougher'n 'e looks. He'll come out fightin'.'

'He alone?' a new voice asked.

There was a long silence. Finally the first voice said, 'Who knows? Be ready though. He's butted inta our territory, hittin' our marks, for the last time. I already warned 'im once. This time we're gonna get rid of 'im.'

As silently as possible, Robert moved to the caved-in side of the room. He felt Pat right behind him. From memory he crawled through charred wood and tangled debris, making his way out the escape route they had devised for just such a time as this.

Behind them they heard the sound of the board being kicked from the window. 'There's a blanket!' someone called.

'Well, jerk it down. Get in there!'

They stopped trying to be quiet, knowing the sounds of the street gang smashing their way into their hideaway would cover their noise. Ahead, Robert could see a break in the darkness. A whiff of fresh air momentarily replaced the stifling smell of smoke and ashes. Then he was out of the ruins on to the sidewalk, almost half a block from the window.

He turned and pulled Pat the last of the way into the clear. He took a deep breath.

'Nice trick, havin' a back way out!'

They whirled to see three members of the street gang standing behind them. One of them lifted his voice and called out, 'They're out here! Here they are!'

Robert charged the speaker. His fist connected with the young man's chin with a sickening thud. The fellow's head snapped backward, and he collapsed without a sound.

Immediately blows began to rain down on Robert from every side. Shoes and knees probed for his groin. He swung with all his might at everything that came within reach, but he and Pat were slowly driven farther apart.

Then he heard a choking, gurgling sound. It was followed immediately by a disembodied voice asking, 'What'd you do?'

The voice Robert recognized as the first one that spoke outside the window replied, 'Stuck 'im! What'dya think?'

There was just an instant of hesitation, even in such a street gang, at the suddenness of a life being snuffed out on the street. In that instant, Robert barreled the body in front of him out of the way, and ran.

The pursuit formed immediately, but he was fast, and he was running for his life. He ducked around obstacles, leaped over fences, dodged between buildings, and fled down any avenue that opened before him. He ran until his breath came in ragged gasps. He flattened against a building and tried to breathe evenly enough to hear.

Slowly his breathing returned to normal. There was no longer any sound of pursuit. He heaved a great sigh. Then he shuddered. The gurgling sounds his friend had made in death echoed in his mind. He shuddered again.

He pushed away from the building and began to walk. Lights of some building became a discernible glow ahead of him. 'Railroad Station,' he informed himself. 'I've seen that before.'

He stood there in indecision for several heart-beats. Then he started trotting toward the station.

As he neared it, he saw a passenger train just ready to leave. The conductor was swinging his lantern in a signal to the engineer.

'Wait a minute!' he called. 'I want on.'

'Hurry it up, then,' the conductor called back. 'We're leavin'.'

The train was already starting to move as Robert swung aboard. The conductor followed him, looking him over carefully. 'You got money to buy a ticket?' the conductor demanded.

Robert nodded. 'Yeah. I've been saving up to get out of New York,' he replied.

'Well, you better cough up enough for a ticket before we get to going too fast,' the conductor shot back. 'It don't feel good to get tossed off the train once we get goin' good.'

Robert grinned suddenly. This, at least, he had an answer for. As he paid for the ticket and got his change, he wondered if he was at all ready for whatever lay ahead.

2

'So where to, son?' the conductor demanded.

'How far does this train go?' Robert shot back.

'A whole lot farther'n you want to go. Or farther than you have money to go.'

'I have money.'

'Then why are you dressed like that? Where'd you get the money? Steal it?'

'No, I didn't steal it,' Robert lied. 'I had to get down to the station at night. I didn't want to be robbed on the way. Best way to keep from getting robbed is to look like you don't have anything.'

'How old are you, son? Twelve? Thirteen?'

Robert grinned. He pushed the soft cap back so his face showed. He shucked off the oversized coat and squared his shoulders. Beneath the coat, his clothes were not that bad. He had learned, over the two years since his family was killed, to steal well. He was dressed as well as someone of at least moderate means.

He bent over and unwrapped the rags from his shoes. He watched, out of the corner of his eye, as the conductor's expression and attitude changed. 'Maybe you did dress that way on purpose,' the conductor mused. 'Where you headin'?'

Robert sighed heavily. 'As far from New York City as I can get.'

'Well, you got the right train, at least. The Union Pacific goes all the way West, and makes connections anywhere you want to go.'

'I'll be needing a job, sooner or later, I suppose,' Robert confessed. 'Where's there work to be had?'

The conductor looked him over appraisingly. 'Well, you're right small built. Ever think about the mines?'

'What mines?'

'The Union Pacific owns and operates coal mines out west. Hard work, but it pays good. I just happen to know about it because my wife has a nephew that went out there. Wyoming Territory.'

'How far is it?'

'Seven days.'

Robert frowned. 'All on the train?'

'All on the train. Oh, it stops at all the towns. Most places you got time to grab a bite to eat, or relieve yourself. 'Course, once you're a ways out you can do that from between the cars most anyplace.'

'Wyoming Territory, huh?'

'Yup. The U.P.'s got mines at Carbon, at Rock Springs, and at Evanston. According to the wife's nephew, Rock Springs is the best one to work at.'

'OK. Sell me a ticket to Rock Springs, Wyoming Territory.'

The conductor figured up the price and made out the ticket. Abruptly he asked, 'What are you running from?'

Robert's head shot up. 'What?'

'What are you running from?'

'I'm not running.'

'Of course you are. You running from the law?'

Robert shook his head. He suddenly felt a need to confide in someone. 'Street

16

gangs, actually.'

'The gangs are after you?'

'Yeah. My family got killed a couple years ago.'

'How'd that happen?'

'Fire. We had an apartment. Fifth floor.'

'Irish section?'

'Why'd you ask that? I don't talk Irish.'

'No, but you look Irish.'

'Yeah. Irish. There were some of them real religious folks lived on the second floor. They were always burning candles to every saint they ever heard of. I suppose their candles started it, but I don't know. Anyway, I woke up in the middle of the night, and there was fire everywhere. I got out my window and shinnied down a drain pipe. It was hot enough I got blisters sliding down it, but it held.'

'The rest of your family weren't so lucky, huh?'

'No. They all died. Couldn't even find their bodies, it was so hot. Burned everything plumb up.'

'So how'd the street gangs get involved?'

Robert sighed. 'I just started living on the street. Couldn't get a job. Too young. Too little. Pat McCormick started teaching me how to steal. Stole enough to get by. Then one of the gangs decided we were working their territory, and tried to run us out. We fought with them. They killed Pat.'

'So where'd you get the money?'

'You ask too many questions. Let's just leave it there.'

The conductor shrugged. 'I don't have any love for the cops,' he said. 'I'm not gonna turn you in.'

'Then how about letting me find a seat?'

'Go right ahead. First decent stop-over you have, I'd advise you to go buy a valise of some kind. Get some extra clothes, a razor, things like that. Then you'll look like a legitimate traveler. It'll save you answering a lot of questions from every conductor that comes on.'

'Thanks,' Robert mumbled.

He made his way to a seat and settled

in for a long trip.

It was a long trip, a very long trip. He had no idea this country was so big. He made enough idle conversation to learn that Wyoming Territory wasn't much over half way across it, and he began to think he would never get that far. By the end of the first night his back and legs hurt. He paced the cars of the train, learning to step across the gap from car to car.

The first two-hour layover he followed the conductor's advice. He bought a valise made of some material like carpet, with paisley print on the sides and leather handles. He bought two sets of clothing, a razor, strop, brush and a cake of lather. Then he occupied himself for nearly half a day learning to strop the razor to a perfect edge. Half a dozen men on the train offered him tips and advice as he worked to develop a stroke and rhythm, trying from memory to copy what he had seen his father do so many times.

That was the first time he had allowed himself to dwell on any memory of his family. He realized suddenly that he had talked about them more the past few days than he had in the past two years. That must mean something, he decided. He just didn't know what.

By the time he got to Rock Springs he hoped he would never see or hear another train. The settled east had given way to open space with well-tended farms and small towns. They crossed small streams and great rivers. The last two days he had seen nothing but sage brush, yucca, cactus, and dust. There were a lot of jackrabbits, occasional buffalo, and frequent herds of pronghorn antelope. There was a coyote once in a while. Once a pack of wolves were feeding on a carcass near the track. They scarcely looked up as the train thundered along.

The most fascinating thing he saw was the cowboys. He saw some of them on their horses, moving vast herds of cattle, keeping them away from the tracks. He saw a few of them as they rode the train from one stop to the next. He saw a few of them as they raced the train, lying low on their horses' necks, pitting the speed of their mount against the great iron monster. They never won. At least, not for long.

'Rock Springs,' the conductor announced, walking through the car. 'We'll be stopped for fifteen minutes.'

Robert stood and stretched his legs. He grabbed his valise and walked to the end of the car. He glanced around and noticed the only other people standing were grouped at the door on the other side of the car. He turned and walked that way, joining the line.

As soon as the train stopped, people poured out of the car as though a cork had been removed from a bottle. Robert stopped on the platform and looked around.

He stared in amazement at a group of Chinese men, huddled together talking animatedly. Their long queues bounced and danced as they bobbed their heads and gestured. 'Chinese?' he breathed to himself. 'Clear out here?'

He shrugged and walked through the train station and on to the main street of

Rock Springs. There had to be some mistake. This wasn't a town. This was just a collection of shacks and corrals, jumbled together with no particular order. There were no sidewalks. Everything seemed coated in a dark dust.

He turned and looked the other way. It wasn't hard to spot the mine. Huge piles of coal slag were abandoned everywhere they could be piled out of the way. The entrance to the mine was marked by a sign that said simply, 'No. 1.'

Away from the town, as far as he could see, other mine entrances loomed as well. He could count five from where he stood. Piles of rock and coal slag made the only break in the rolling plains.

He shrugged his shoulders and walked toward the building beside the entrance marked 'No. 1.'

He stepped inside and waited for his eyes to adjust to the dim interior. As they did he made out a desk. Behind the desk, a scrawny man with glasses perched on his nose eyed him. 'Can I help you?' he asked.

'Uh, yeah. I was looking for a job.'

'You a miner?'

'No. I can learn, though.'

'Ever handle a jackleg?'

'A what?'

'Never mind. You just answered me. Ever handle dynamite?'

'No.'

'Ever been underground?'

'No.'

'You stouter'n you look?'

'Yes.'

'How old are you?'

'Twenty,' Robert lied.

'Twenty, goin' on fifteen?'

'Twenty going on nineteen,' Robert corrected.

'Little for your age.'

'Big for my size though,' Robert shot back.

The clerk chuckled. 'Lots o' good miners is little,' he observed. 'Seems to help some. You write?'

'Sure.'

' 'Tain't that sure out here. Half the fellas that come in here can't. Here. Fill this out.'

Robert took the extended pencil and filled in the information. 'I don't have an address.'

'Where you stayin'?'

'I'm not, yet.'

'You got money?'

'Some.'

'Then stay over at the Swensons' Boarding House. If you ain't got money, you kin stay at the company boardin' house, but you don't wanta stay there.'

'So am I hired?'

'You're hired. Start tomorrow. Second shift. You start at three in the afternoon. Be here at two. You need boots, not them fancy shoes. Tough clothes, too. Not them city duds. You need a pick, miner's hat, sledge an' a eighteen pound drill or two.'

'Where do I get those?'

'If you got money, you can get 'em at the Mercantile Store. Spauldings carry everything. If you ain't, you kin get 'em at the company store. They'll be took off yore first check. And the second. And the third. I'll give you a piece of advice. If you got money, go to Spauldings. Unless you're one o' them rat-eatin' pagans, the company store'll charge you three prices for everything you get.'

'What do you mean?'

The clerk sighed. He assumed the pose of a lecturing professor. 'It's this way. The U.P. imports all them heathen Chinese to work the mines. They favor 'em over white men, 'cause they work cheaper, work longer hours, don't have no respect for their own lives, an' won't join unions. So the U.P. gives 'em their stuff for half what they sell it to whites for.'

'That don't seem right.'

'Right ain't got nothin' to do with it. The rail-road's god out here, son. You take what they do, or go back east.'

'Well, I guess I'll go up to Spauldings to get my stuff, then.'

'Smart fella.'

'Where is it?'

'Go back into town and follow the main street. Second street that goes north, you go north too. You'll see it on your right. They got a sign.'

'Thanks. Where do I report for work?'

'Right over there at the entrance to No. 1. Your name'll be on the roster.'

'Guess I better buy myself a watch, too,' Robert said to himself as he walked back toward town. 'Otherwise I'll never know when it's time to go to work.'

Something in the pit of his stomach told him he had just entered a whole new world. He didn't know it yet, but he wouldn't like it. He would not like it one bit.

3

'Hi. Can I help you?'

Robert blinked his eyes several times. His tongue seemed stuck to the roof of his mouth. He opened and closed his mouth several times. He stared into the smiling face before him as into some strange apparition.

'Is something wrong?' the same melodic voice asked.

His tongue abruptly came unglued. 'No. Nothing. Absolutely nothing, as far as I can see,' he said. 'I'm sorry. I was standing there like a tongue-tied wharf rat. I didn't expect to see anything that beautiful in my whole lifetime.'

Sissy Spaulding flushed prettily. She bravely tried to maintain a clerk/customer demeanor. 'Can I help you with something?' she repeated.

'You already have,' Robert assured her. 'Since I left New York City, I've been trying to think of one really good reason for heading West. Just being able to see you standing there is a good enough reason for the whole trip.'

'You, you're from New York City?' she echoed.

'Yes, Ma'am. Born and bred there. Never set foot out of the city until I got on that train headed West.'

'Why on earth did you come here?'

'I wasn't sure until I saw you.'

'Stop it! You're embarrassing me.'

'I know. And every time I do, you blush like that, and it makes you even more beautiful. My name is Robert Purdy. At your service, Ma'am.'

He pulled off his cap and made a sweeping bow.

Sissy giggled. 'I've never had anyone introduce himself like that! I'm Sissy Spaulding.'

'Sissy?' Robert asked. 'I dare say that's short for something.'

She blushed again. 'It's short for Narcissa.'

'Aha!' he said. 'Named after a Greek

god. A fit name in fact for a goddess. So much more beautiful than Sissy.'

Sissy giggled again. 'But it works a lot better around here. Can you imagine people around here trying to say "Narcissa"?'

'Narcissa,' he breathed. 'I can't think of anything easier to say.'

She tried again to gain control of the conversation. 'And what can I do for you, Mr smooth talking Robert Purdy?'

'Marry me,' Robert said instantly.

'What?!'

'Marry me,' he repeated.

'I don't even know you!'

'Of course you do. I just introduced myself.'

'So I know your name. I still don't know *you*.'

'So ask me anything you want. I will answer you honestly and simply, so that you may get to know me as well as you like.'

'I'd rather just sell you what you came here to buy.'

Robert sighed melodramatically. 'Ah, well. Then I guess that will have to do for now. But you will marry me, Narcissa Spaulding.'

'What makes you think so?'

'I just know it. I knew it the instant I saw you. What's your middle name?'

'Whitman.'

'Whitman?'

'Whitman.'

'What kind of name is that? Narcissa is a name as beautiful as you. Spaulding is your family name, of course. What kind of name is Whitman?'

She giggled again. 'I was named for the first white woman to cross South Pass. Her name was Narcissa Whitman, and she's kind of my mother's hero.'

'Heroine.'

'What?'

'Heroine. A man is a hero. The feminine form is heroine.'

'Oh. I didn't know that. You must be educated.'

'I went to one of the best schools in New York City. All the way through the tenth grade.'

'That's a long way. I went through the

eighth grade.'

'That's far enough,' he assured her. 'Especially if you don't stop reading and learning.'

'Oh, I read as much as I can,' she responded. 'It's a little hard to get books here, but Papa always includes at least one for me in every order of goods for the store.'

'Ah, that answers my next question.'

'Which was?'

'Whether the store is your father's.'

'So now you already know. Now, what can I sell you in my father's store, Robert Purdy?'

'Well, I have a list. I just hired on at the mine.'

'You're going to mine?'

The disappointment in her voice stabbed him like a knife. 'What's wrong with that?'

'Oh, nothing, really. It's just such a dirty, dangerous job. Then there's the trouble with the Chinese. That's going to boil over one of these days.'

'I picked up some on that at the mine

office,' he admitted. 'The guy that hired me didn't sound too keen on the "rat-eating pagans" I think he called them.'

She giggled again. 'That's one of the nice things they're called. So you need a six-pound pick, a three-pound sledge, an eighteen-pound drill, boots, pants, and miner's cap?'

'Hey, you read my whole list.'

'At least you're not buying them from the Union Pacific.'

'I heard they're high.'

'Three times a fair price,' she agreed. 'Like everything else they sell their own workers.'

'Well, it'll do till I find a better job,' he offered.

She looked at him closely. 'Have you considered working on a ranch?'

'A ranch? I wouldn't know anything at all about that. I saw some cowboys from the train on the way out. They're different!'

She giggled again. He loved the sound of that giggle! 'Some of them are just wild, reckless men that live hard and die young,' she explained. 'But some of them save their money, homestead on a good piece of land, and build up a nice ranch.'

'Really? You can do that?'

'Sure, if you work hard.'

'Wow! To own real land! Now that would be something!'

At a loss for an answer, she turned and began to assemble the things on his list. She didn't ask what he needed. It was apparent that it was a common thing to outfit a new miner. When she had the pile of things put together, she said, 'That'll be twenty one dollars and seven cents.'

He whistled. 'Quite a bit.'

She nodded. 'But if you bought it from the Union Pacific, it'd take you three months to pay for it.'

He paid for the purchases. 'Now then, is there a place in town where I could ask the most beautiful girl I have ever met to have supper with me?'

She blushed again. 'No.'

'No?'

'No. There are some places to eat,

that cater to miners or cowboys. They're saloons, mostly. I wouldn't set foot in one of them.'

'How about Swenson's Boarding House?'

'Is that where you're living?'

'Where I intend to. I haven't been there yet.'

'Then you better go do that first. You can worry about all your smooth talk later.'

'Well, then, when I get my room taken care of, and get settled in a little, will you have supper with me?'

'We'll see,' she said.

'Is that a yes?'

'That's a "We'll see".'

'Oh. Then I will be back to see, Narcissa Spaulding.'

He picked up the bundle into which she had tied his purchases. With the other hand he grabbed the valise he had left beside the door. He flashed her his very best smile as he went out the door. Her answering smile warmed him all the way through.

4

'But if I did that, I would never get to see you.'

Sissy stared hard into Robert's eyes. She sighed heavily. 'I know. That bothers me a lot, too. The past two months have been the happiest days of my life. I never thought I could feel about anybody like I feel about you.'

'So why do you want me to leave town?'

'I don't,' she said honestly. 'I don't really want you out of my sight. Every day I wait until your shift is over and I know you'll be stopping by. Even if you don't go to the boarding house and clean up first, you're the most wonderful thing in the world to look at.'

'You think so? You ought to see you through my eyes.'

She reddened noticeably, even in the fading light, as she ignored his comment.

'But the fact is,' she continued, 'Papa would never even consider letting us get married as long as you're working in the mine.'

'It doesn't pay as good as it sounded,' he agreed. 'I actually have less money now than I did when I hired out. And I buy my supplies from you. I can't imagine how fellows make it that have to buy their stuff at the company store. And I'm getting to where I can't hardly stand it down there. I feel like the whole Earth's on top of me. And the dust seeps into my eyes and nose and throat. Even after I get off work, my whole insides have to be black for hours. I spit, and it's black. I blow my nose, and it's black. I cough, and the stuff I cough up is black. No matter how much or how long I wash, I can't get the black out of the lines in my skin or around my finger nails. I hate it! If they'd put in more fans, the air would at least be better down there, but the U.P. acts like they don't care a bit.'

The porch swing they were seated on, suspended from the ceiling of the

Spaulding's front porch, stopped its motion. Bitterness gave her voice a hard edge. 'They don't. Every month most of the miners are deeper in debt to the company. After a while, the Union Pacific practically owns their soul. It'd be different without the Chinese. They're willing to work so many hours, and work so hard. It's almost impossible to match what they bring out of the ground. And the company favors them so much. I'm really afraid of what's going to happen, one of these days.'

'Me too,' Robert admitted. 'There's a lot of talk of getting rid of the Chinese completely, one way or another. I've seen what that can lead to. The street gangs tried that with each other in the city. The Nativists were pitted against the Immigrants, and there was never an end to it. I was an immigrant, even though I was born in the city. My folks came over from Ireland, so that decided what side I was on. The gangs try to kill off the other side all the time. They just keep on killing each other to get even with the other gang for killing one of theirs, that was killed to get even for killing someone else. Nobody even remembers where it started. There's always just one more that has to be avenged, then that vengeance has to be avenged, and it never stops.'

'That's another reason you need to get away,' she insisted. 'It's getting close to spring. If you go now, you can probably hire on to one of the ranches, even without having any experience, they're always so desperate for hands through calving, they'll hire you. Then, as hard as you work, and as strong and quick as you are, they'll be willing to teach you what you need to know.'

'Yeah, but then what?' he pressed.

'Then you can start saving your money, so you can buy a few cows. Then you can homestead on a piece of ground to get a start.'

'But that'll take so long!' he lamented. 'I can't wait that kind of time. That'd mean it'd be years before I could even ask you to marry me.'

'You asked me that the first day I met you.'

He grinned. 'Well, I mean before I'd dare ask your father.'

'Not necessarily.'

'What do you mean?'

'It doesn't have to take years,' she insisted. 'You just need to learn how to ranch. How to take care of cows. How to calve. How to train horses. All those things. As soon as you think you know enough to start your own place, you can homestead. If Papa lets us get married, I can homestead one quarter section, and you the quarter next to it. We can homestead near good water, so we can graze on all the land around it.'

'Graze what? I don't have any cows, and I don't have enough money left to buy more than two or three.'

'But I have some money saved up. It's not enough, but if you can not spend any money for a year or so, at the end of a year with your savings and mine, it would be enough to get a start.'

They were both silent for a long moment, staring into their dreams. They were interrupted from a voice within the house. 'Gettin' awful quiet out there.'

Sissy giggled. 'Oh, Papa,' she called back. 'We're just thinking. He isn't even holding my hand!'

The voice from the house called out, 'Well, why isn't he?'

Sissy giggled again, but it was Robert's ebullient nature that responded. 'Because she has so many coats on I don't know what pocket she has her hands in.'

Norman Spaulding's booming laugh carried well beyond the porch. 'Well, you could always sit in the parlor, you know.'

'Promise not to listen to our conversation?' Robert shot back.

'I ain't promisin' nothin',' Norman responded. 'I ain't even promised not to listen in through the door when you're out there.'

'Oh, Papa,' Sissy protested.

'You had best be comin' in the house,' Norman said. 'You'll be catchin' your death o' cold out there, even if it is unseasonable warm. It's still February, you know.'

'I know. I'll be in, in a minute.'

There was another period of silence. It was Robert who broke it. 'How would I go about it?'

'Go about what?'

'Getting a job on a ranch.'

She shrugged her shoulders. 'Go to one of them and ask.'

'But they're way off somewhere. I don't have any way to get there.'

Silence settled over them again, then she sat up abruptly. 'There's a spur line that runs up a ways into the mountains.'

He nodded. 'It supplies those little mines up there. I asked about that track. They don't take passengers, though.'

'Oh. I didn't think about that.'

'Of course, I could slip on to one of the cars.'

'Sneak on?'

'Sure. Then I could watch, and when I see a ranch that looks likely, I could just bail off of the train. But if they didn't hire me, I'd have an awful long walk anywhere else.'

'Oh, they wouldn't just make you walk off,' she insisted. 'Nobody in this country would do that. They'd at least let you stay in the bunkhouse until someone was going to another ranch, or to town, with a buck-board or something. Then you could ride along.'

The silence thickened for a long while again. 'Will you keep my stuff?' he asked.

'You're going to go?'

'Well, sure. If that's what I have to do so we can get married, I'll go tonight.'

'Tonight?'

'Sure. Why not?'

'But that's so soon.'

'The sooner I leave, the sooner I can come back. You will wait for me, won't you?'

Even in the semi-darkness he could see the deep emotion in her eyes. He felt as if he was sinking helplessly and hopelessly into them. She came into his arms. 'Oh, Robert! I would wait for you till the end of time.'

Their lips found each other's, brimming with passion and hope and promise. The spell was broken by Norman's voice again. 'Sissy! You do need to come in.'

She pulled away from Robert reluctantly. 'Coming, Papa.'

'I'll drop my stuff off in about an hour.'

'At least eat supper first.'

He sighed. 'Can't stand to. If I see you in the light, I won't be able to go at all. I'll leave now. I'll just put my stuff on the porch later.'

Without waiting for an answer he couldn't deal with, he plunged off the porch and strode away.

Two hours later he quietly sat a large bundle on the porch. His mining tools he laid quietly beside it. Clinging to the valise he had purchased en route from New York, he headed for the train he had already noticed. On the spur line he and Sissy had talked about, there was a short train getting ready to pull out. He hurried to catch it.

Approaching the train, he noticed a dozen empty ore cars and two box cars. He slipped quietly along the train, checking the box cars. Their doors were padlocked shut. He swore under his breath.

A lantern from beside the caboose

swung back and forth in a wide arc. In response, the engine emitted a puff of steam. The cars banged and clanked as the slack was taken out of the couplings. It started to move.

Robert swore. He looked back and forth, squinting into the darkness. He started walking quickly along the track, hurrying to find a car he could climb into. The train began to pick up speed. It was soon moving as fast as he was walking. He began to trot. Swearing softly again, he tossed his valise into an ore car. Catching the top rim of the car with both hands, he leaped up, swinging his legs upward.

He caught the top of the car with a heel, and hauled himself up and over the side. He dropped down into the darkness, landing with a thud on the steel floor of the car. Coal dust kicked up around him.

He swore again. 'Wouldn't you know I'd pick a coal car! Well, what else would be on a train goin' to a coal mine?'

Already lying flat, he knew he was as dirty as he was going to get. He chuckled suddenly. 'What a way to start a new life!'

he told himself. 'Not much better than last time. Well, it is, though. Nobody's chasing me, trying to kill me. Besides, this time I have something to work for. This time I'm coming back. Oh, Sissy! I can't wait.'

He closed his eyes. He willed himself to adjust his body to the rough swaying of the iron car. He drifted off to sleep with surprising ease.

5

Bright sunlight peeked over the edge of the ore car, bathing Robert's face in brightness. He squinted and stirred, shielding his eyes with a hand. Remembering his surroundings, he moved slowly to his feet, trying not to stir up any more coal dust than necessary. He took a deep breath. The air felt sharp and clean.

He stretched to peer over the side of the car. Before him a world stretched away into the distance without any sign of habitation. Rolling hills dotted with sage brush reached endlessly. In the distance he could make out dark shapes he was sure were animals. He had no idea what kind.

The train swayed to one side. He shifted his weight to keep from tumbling across to bang against the black side of the car. 'Going around a bend,' he informed himself.

He turned and looked in the direction the train was moving. He could see the black smoke from the locomotive drifting along the train, breaking up in the steady breeze. Ahead, mountains loomed. He gasped.

'Mountains! I've heard of mountains out here. Didn't see any on the way out, but they say it's plumb cold in the mountains, clear into June.'

The thought made the cold he already felt stab through him. He shivered and pulled his coat closer around his shoulders. 'Best find some place to get off this thing before we get there,' he said aloud.

He moved to the other side of the car and peered over the side. His heart leaped. 'That's a town!' he said.

He stared for several minutes, then corrected himself. 'Too small for a town. I wonder if that's a ranch. Too far away to tell. Must be two or three miles.'

He looked ahead up the tracks. As he did, the pitch of the car changed noticeably. At once the train began to slow.

'Going up a hill,' he said.

He looked into the distance at the ranch again. He sighed heavily. 'Well, I guess that's as good a place to start as any. Sure hope I don't end up having to walk all the way back to Rock Springs.'

The train slowed to a crawl. Smoke poured from the locomotive. He grabbed his valise and tossed it over the side of the car. Then he grabbed the side of the car and hauled himself up. He perched precariously on the lip of the car, looking for a spot to land.

The track was bedded on large gravel that reached three feet beyond the end of the ties. Beyond the gravel was sage brush, grass and yucca. Nothing looked very soft. Taking a deep breath, he catapulted himself from the side of the car, being sure to jump far enough to escape the gravel.

It seemed a long way to the ground. He landed on the unyielding earth and pitched forward. He tucked his shoulder and rolled, coming to a stop against a clump of sage brush. Half a dozen sage hens broke from the clump of brush with a thunder of wings.

Robert gasped and flung his hands up in front of his face. He watched the birds fly away, then grinned. 'Half scared me to death!' he said aloud. 'Wonder what kind of birds they are.'

He picked himself up and began trying to brush the coal dust from his clothes. He was only moderately successful. He looked at his hands. They were as black as the coal he had spent the past several weeks mining.

'Bet my face is just as bad,' he guessed.

He looked around for anything he could use to clean himself up. Spotting a tall clump of grass, he pulled a handful of it. He wiped it across his face and looked at it. As he expected, it came away black. There were piles of snow against the north side of almost every clump of sage brush. He picked up handfuls of it and used it to wash with, shivering with cold as he did so. He spent the better part of thirty minutes, then, pulling grass and using it to dry with, and to wipe as much of the remaining coal from his hands, face and clothes as he could. Then he sighed. 'Guess that's as good as I'm going to do without water,' he conceded.

He walked back along the tracks until he found his valise. He checked it over. It seemed none the worse for wear. He looked for the ranch he had spotted, and saw it at once. He started for it, walking jauntily.

An hour later his confident expression began to change. The ranch seemed no closer than it had when he left the railroad track. He knew he could walk three miles in an hour on a city street. He had to be able to walk at least half that fast across the open country. Yet he didn't seem to be making any progress at all.

A coyote burst from a shallow draw just as he stepped off its ledge to start across it. He yelled and dropped his valise. 'That was a wolf!' he said. 'Well, at least he ran from me, instead of trying to eat me.'

He waited for his hammering heart to slow, then picked up the valise and resumed his walk. It was nearly noon when he staggered into the ranch yard, footsore and thoroughly confused. The sign over the front gate said, 'Eden Valley Cattle Company'. The brand 'EV' was burned into the wood at both ends of the sign. The ranch dogs were barking frantically. He stopped in the middle of the yard, completely uncertain what direction to go, or what to do.

An old cowboy stepped out the door of the blacksmith shop and spotted him. He stared for a long moment, then turned and called over his shoulder. 'Hey, Frank! Come lookit what wandered in.'

Another cowboy that Robert didn't see a way to distinguish from the first stepped out and joined the other. He turned his head and spit a brown stream at the ground, then studied Robert again. Then he walked across the yard to where Robert waited.

'Howdy,' he said.

'Uh, hello,' Robert replied.

'You lookin' fer someone?'

'Uh, no. No. Actually, I'm looking for a job. Uh, my name is Robert Purdy.'

'You don't look like a Robert Purdy.'

'Pardon me?'

'I said you don't look like no Robert Purdy. You look like some bedraggled runt out've a coyote's litter what got drug through the coal box. Where you from, Robert Purdy?'

'New York.'

'New York City?'

'Yes sir.'

'How in tarnation did you git clear out here from New York City? That's clear back East.'

'Uh, yes, it is. I, uh, I rode the train. I, uh, I came out to Rock Springs to work in the mine, but I didn't like the mine very well.'

'Looks like ya jist crawled out've it. How long did you stick with it?'

'Two and a half months, I guess.'

Just then the cook stepped out of the cook house and began clanging an iron triangle with a steel rod. Men appeared as if by magic from all directions, heading for the cook house.

Frank Ritter spat another stream of

tobacco juice at the ground. 'Well, Robert Purdy, why don't you wash up with the boys and we'll have a bite to eat. Then we'll talk.'

Gratitude washed through Robert. He hadn't realized until that moment how hungry he was. He remembered suddenly that he hadn't eaten for twenty four hours, and he was famished. He hurried to the line of cowboys washing up on the porch of the cook house.

When it was his turn he used plenty of the strong soap and turned three wash basins of water black before he satisfied himself he was clean enough to eat. He was keenly aware of the cowboys openly staring at him, but none of them offered any conversation, so he held his silence as well.

He stepped on into the cook house and eyed the long table, with benches along both sides. He felt a sudden rush of gratitude for the time spent at Swenson's Boarding House. Before that time, he had no idea how to eat in a group of rough, working men. He quickly learned that to wait for anything to be passed was to wait with an empty plate, but to stand and stretch across the table instead of asking for something to be passed was to get a hand rapped with whatever was handy. He also learned that those who ate quickly usually managed to have seconds, but there was seldom anything left for those who ate slowly.

He didn't have to force himself to eat quickly. The food was tasty and substantial. It tasted like some manna of the gods. He wolfed three plates of it down before he even bothered to become aware of the others at the table. As he swallowed the last bite of that third plateful, he noticed everyone at the table staring at him.

He looked around quickly. No malice showed in any face, only curiosity. 'Where'd you find the runt, Frank?'

'It wasn't in the chuck wagon,' another suggested. 'I don't think he's had a square meal in a while.'

'Shore put a bait of it away anyway,' another agreed.

'Where you from, Runt?' a fourth man

called.

'Uh, New York,' Robert offered.

'New York City?'

'Yes sir.'

'What in thunder you doin' clear out here?'

'Says he wants a job,' Frank explained.

Laughter erupted around the table. Robert's ears burned suddenly. 'What's funny about that?' he demanded.

'Job doin' what?' an old cowboy queried. 'We got no street cars to scrub.'

'I want to learn how to be a cowboy,' Robert responded.

Laughter broke out again, as though he had said something hilariously funny. He bristled. 'I still don't see what's funny about that.'

'Ever been on a horse, Runt?'

'Well, no.'

'Ever throw a rope?'

'No.'

'Ever have a lariat in your hand?'

'No.'

'Ever see one throwed?'

'Well, yes. On the train, coming out. I

watched a cowboy rope a cow.'

'Looked plumb simple, did it?'

'Well, yes. It didn't look all that difficult. He whirled it around and threw it. The loop just dropped right over the cow's head.'

Laughter greeted the observation. 'All by itself, it did,' the old one observed.

Robert looked around from face to face. Understanding began to seep into him that this was a different and foreign world he knew nothing of. The denizens of this world were fiercely proud of their knowledge and skills. It was a brazen affront that this city boy could wander in and assume he could become one of them.

'I didn't know anything about mining coal when I got to Rock Springs,' he offered. 'But I learned quick. I was loading more than any white man on my shift by the end of the first month. I'm a whole lot stronger than I look, and I do learn fast. All I'm asking is a chance to learn.'

'And if I don't hire you, what're you gonna do?' Frank demanded.

Robert sighed. 'Then I'll just have to

ask the way to the next ranch, and start walking.'

'You'd walk to the next ranch?'

He shrugged. 'That's the way I got here.'

'Where'd you walk from?'

'The railroad.'

'That spur line up to South Pass?'

'I guess so. It turned and started up toward the mountains. I spotted this ranch, so I bailed out and walked here. The car I hitched a ride in was a coal car. That's why I got so dirty.'

'You walked here from the big bend o' the tracks?'

He nodded.

'That's ten er twelve miles.'

'No wonder it seemed so far! I thought it was a couple miles when I started. But it took me all day, from sunup till I got here, to walk it.'

'I ain't walked that far in the last six months,' a cowboy observed.

'Don't plan to in the next six months neither,' another agreed.

'You on the run?' Frank asked abruptly.

Robert sighed again. 'No. I was. I'm not now.'

'Who was you on the run from?'

'Nativists.'

'Who?'

'One of the gangs in the city. My folks were Irish. That makes me an immigrant, in the city. There's gangs there. The Nativists are one gang. They didn't like me operating in their territory, and they tried to kill me. They killed my friend. Stabbed him. I fought my way loose, made it to the railroad station, and hopped the train. The conductor told me there were jobs in the mine, so I came out to Rock Springs.'

'You got folks?'

'No. They're all dead. Died in a fire.'

Silence met the explanation, as each man weighed Robert's words. It was the foreman who spoke. 'Sort of like starting a new life or somethin', huh?'

'Something like that.'

It was exactly like that, Robert knew. How new that life would be, he had no way to know.

6

Mack Anderson shook his head. 'I gotta have rocks in my head.'

'I sure do appreciate you being willing to teach me to be a cowboy,' Robert assured him.

Mack bristled. 'Now listen here, Runt. I ain't nothin' o' the kind! I'm hirin' ya on as a hand. I know ya don't know what end o' the horse to get on, but I ain't offerin' to make my foreman no school teacher. I shore ain't takin' ya ta raise! It's up to you to learn what ya gotta learn, an' we'll see if you're man enough to learn it, in spite of bein' the runt o' whatever litter you come outa. I'll give ya fair time to learn, but no more'n what's fair. If ya don't start pullin' yore own weight in a month er two, I'll tie a can ta yore tail so fast it'll make yore head swim.'

'Oh, you won't be sorry.'

'I ain't gonna be sorry either way,' the

rancher growled. 'Either you break in good an' make a good hand, or you don't an' you get sent packin'. Either way it ain't no skin off my butt. I don't s'pose you got any outfit.'

'Outfit?'

'Outfit,' Mack repeated. 'Rig. Saddle. Decent duds to work in. The sorta stuff any workin' cowpoke's gotta have.'

'Uh, no. No, I don't. I bought mining gear, but I left it at Rock Springs. Stored it with, with some folks.'

'Well, you'll be needin' an outfit.'

'Where do I get that?'

'The general store in town, o' course. Farson's about ten, twelve miles. I'll be sendin' in after supplies tomorrow. Ya kin ride the buck-board in. Get you some duds. Don't ferget the chaps, an' a pair o' spurs. Just tell Isaac you're hirin' on with me, an' you ain't got one dang thing. He'll outfit you.'

Robert cleared his throat. 'I, uh, don't, I mean, I'm not sure I have enough money left to do that with. How much will all that cost? I spent most of my money getting outfitted to mine.'

'That figures. Don't matter none. You don't need the money. Tell Isaac you're hirin' on with me. He'll outfit you, and put it on the ranch's tab. I'll take it outa your wages. You'll work fer nothin', for three er four months, but you'll get outfitted. Don't ferget the boots, neither. You ain't gonna work fer me wearin' them shoes. I ain't fond o' pickin' up the pieces o' hands what get drug to death, cause they get hung up in a stirrup.'

'I, well, uh, OK. I guess. Thank you!'

The rancher continued. 'Then you go over to Sweaty Miller's saddle shop. You have him fit you out with a saddle. Get you a good all-around workin' saddle an' a bridle, er a hackamore, whatever you like. Same as with Isaac. Tell 'im the ranch'll stand good for it.'

'OK. They'll do that?'

' 'Course they'll do that. Why wouldn't they?'

'Uh, nothing. I'm just not accustomed to business being done that way. In … well, anyway, thank you. I'll do that.'

The sun was just peeking over the mountains the next morning when Robert and Smitty left the ranch yard. They sat side by side on the seat of the buck-board, pulled by a matched pair of nondescript brown Morgans. 'Tell me 'bout New York City,' Smitty said as they left the yard.

Robert shrugged. 'What do you want to know?'

'What's it like, livin' there? Lot's o' people, I 'spect.'

'Yeah, there are a lot of people. Even at night, there are some people on the streets. Mostly people you don't want to meet, though.'

'You born there?'

'Yeah.'

'What's your pa do?'

'Did. He's dead. He worked on the waterfront. Unloading ships, things like that.'

'Dead, huh? Sorry 'bout that. How'd 'e die?'

'He was killed in a fire. My whole family were.'

'Is that a fact? Tough break. You made it out, huh?'

'Yeah. I shinnied down a drain pipe.'

'So how come you come West?'

'I, well, it doesn't matter I guess. How much do I have to learn to be a cowboy?'

Smitty chuckled. 'Well now, that's sorta like askin' what you gotta learn to be the pope. Depends on where you're startin' from. For you, a whole lot, I 'spect.'

'Is riding a horse hard to do? It looks easy.'

Smitty's eyes twinkled. 'Oh, there ain't nothin' to that. Second nature, after while. You jist gotta keep yore feet in the stirrups an' your rear end in the saddle.'

'I saw a horse bucking in the, the, corral, is it?'

'Yup.'

'It didn't look that difficult. The cowboy just sat in the saddle and the horse jumped around a lot.'

Smitty turned his head and seemed to have a fit of coughing. When he could speak he said, 'You're plumb right. Nothin' to it, really. You just sit in the saddle an' let the horse jump around. After while he gets plumb tired o' jumpin' around, and commences to doin' what you want 'im to. It's pertneart as easy as huntin' jackalopes.'

'Jackalopes? What are jackalopes?'

'Well now, they's a cross betwixt jack-rabbits an' antelope.'

'They cross-breed?'

'Well, they ain't s'posed to, but they do, now an' then. Jackalopes is bigger'n jack-rabbits, by quite a bit, but a lot smaller'n antelopes. They're plumb shy, too.'

'Shy?'

'Shy,' Smitty repeated. 'They only come out at night. Full moon is best, 'cause you kin see 'em, you know. One o' these first clear nights, when it's good 'n cold, we'll take you out jackalope huntin'. Let you bag a couple of 'em.'

'Why? Are they good eating?'

'Oh, they're the finest eatin' there is! There ain't nothin' in this world beats jackalope meat. If you stay out all night long, an' plumb freeze your behind off a-waitin' fer one of 'em to show up, it's plumb worth it.'

'How do you hunt them?'

64

'Now that's the trick, it is. You find a good spot, where they got a sorta trail. Takes a good eye to see their trails, it does, but most of us old hands kin see it OK. Then you set up there along their trail with a gunny sack.'

'Gunny sack? You don't shoot them?'

'Oh, no! You wouldn't wanta go shootin' when you're jackalope huntin'. You'll scare every other jackalope outa the country, an' they'll stay hid night 'n day for a month or more. No, you jist wait real quiet an' still till they come along, then you clap that gunny sack clown over 'em, an' tie it up tight. Then you grab another gunny sack an' wait fer the next one.'

'How do you get them to keep coming by the same place?'

'Well, now, that there's where you got to have a good partner. The other feller, you see, slips out around. Way around. An' he gets around on the other side o' the hill, and then he jist starts walkin' back an' forth. Then all the jackalopes in the area'll head over to a different draw to feed. Since they always use the same path, they'll jist come right past ya.'

'Wow! I've never heard of anything like that.'

'Oh, pertneart everyone 'round these parts has hunted jackalopes, time to time. We'll get ya set up to do that first clear, cold full moon we get. You jist gotta remember, though. No matter how cold 'n stiff ya git, you gotta hold real still an' just stay there an' wait. You'll come up empty, shore's anything, if you move around, er if you don't wait long enough.'

'I'll remember that.'

The rest of the way to town they chatted about ranch life, and Smitty did offer Robert some facts and suggestions that would be of great value to him. When they tied up the team in front of the saloon, Smitty announced he was going to have a quick drink before they started loading supplies. Robert declined the offer to join him, and walked straight to the general store.

'What can I help you with?'

Robert cleared his throat. 'Uh, I'm looking for a Mr Isaac.'

The store keeper smiled slightly. 'I'm Isaac. Can I help you?'

'Uh, yes. My name is Robert Purdy. I, I've been hired by Mr Anderson to work on the ranch.'

'Mack hired a greenhorn? Where you from, son?'

'New York.'

'New York City?'

'Yes sir.'

'And Mack hired you for a ranch hand?'

'Yes sir. I, uh, I guess I need, uh, I think Mr Anderson called it an outfit.'

'All right. What all do you need?'

'I'm afraid I have no idea whatever.'

'You've never worked as a cowpoke?'

'No.'

'How'd a New York City boy end up clear out here?'

'Well, I came out to work in the mine at Rock Springs. But I didn't like being underground.'

'Don't blame you a bit for that. So Mack hired you on? How'd you get to the EV?'

'EV?'

'The ranch. That's their brand.'

'Brand? Oh, you mean that mark on their cows? I wondered what that was.'

Isaac eyed the strangest customer his store had seen. 'You are green!' he said. 'Yeah, every outfit ... every ranch, that is, has a brand. They put it on all their livestock, so someone else can't steal them and sell them.'

'How do they put it on there?'

'With a brandin' iron. They got an iron, or irons, that the blacksmith makes for 'em. They heat the iron in a fire and stick it on the cows or calves. It burns the mark into the hide, and it stays there for as long as the animal lives.'

Robert frowned. 'Doesn't that hurt them?'

'Oh, they beller some,' Isaac smiled. 'They get over it real quick, though, if it's done right. Now then, let's get you started here.'

'Oh,' Robert interrupted. 'Before you start getting things, Mr Anderson said ... . I mean, well, I don't have much money. Mr Anderson said to tell you the ranch would stand good for it. Is that all right with you?'

Isaac nodded. 'That's normal,' he said. 'Now, then, let's start with a good hat, then neckerchiefs. Then maybe two or three shirts. Trousers. Chaps. Gloves. Boots. Spurs. What kinda rowels you like?'

'What kind of what?'

'Rowels. What kind of rowels you want on your spurs?'

'I don't have any slightest notion. What are rowels?'

The shopkeeper chuckled again. 'I keep forgetting how green you are. That's the little wheels on the end o' the spurs. That's the part that hits the horse when you spur him. Do you want the kind that'll gouge 'im good and hard, or do you want the kind that'll be a little more gentle, or just mostly to hook in the cinch when your horse is buckin'?'

'I … I have no idea. What would you suggest?'

Isaac pursed his lips. Without answering, he selected a pair of spurs, handing them to Robert. By the time Smitty left the saloon and came in, Isaac had selected a complete wardrobe for a working cowboy, a lariat, saddle-blankets and bedroll, complete with a ground tarp. Robert quietly hoped he could remember what everything was called and used for by the time he got back to the ranch.

'Got all your stuff?' Smitty asked.

'I think so. I, uh, left it up to Isaac.'

'He'll steer ya straight,' Smitty assured him. 'Why don't you hustle over ta Sweaty's an' get ya a saddle an' bridle whilst I get the rest o' our stuff here. I'll jist toss your stuff in the buck-board with the rest.'

Nodding, Robert walked across the street to the saddle shop he had already spotted on his way to the general store. He had the strange feeling of just having had the conversation that ensued.

As he walked in the front door, the saddle maker looked up from the piece of leather he was working on. 'Howdy. What can I do for you?'

'Uh, my name is Robert Purdy. I've

been hired by Mr Anderson to work on the ranch.'

'Mack hired a greenhorn? Where you from, son?'

'New York.'

'New York City?'

'Yes sir.'

'And Mack hired you for a ranch hand?'

'Yes sir. I guess I need a saddle and bridle. Mr Anderson said the ranch would stand good for it.'

'All right. What all do you need?'

'A saddle and bridle, I think.'

Sweaty chuckled. 'Yeah, I sorta figgered that all right. What kinda saddle you want? A-frame, McClellan, Teton?'

'I'm afraid I have no idea, whatever.'

'Well, do you want heavy swells, or light? High cantle or low? What kinda nubbin?'

'I'm sorry. I don't have any idea what those things even mean.'

'You've never worked as a cowpoke?'

'No.'

'How'd a New York City boy end up

71

clear out here?'

'Well, I came out to work in the mine at Rock Springs. But I didn't like being underground.'

'Don't blame you a bit for that. So Mack hired you on? How'd you get to the EV?'

'I hitched a ride on the train, until I could see the ranch. Then I walked from there.'

'That's a good walk. Train track don't get no closer'n ten miles to the EV.'

'It was a lot farther than it looked like.'

Sweaty took a deep breath, looking Robert over carefully. 'Well, if you don't know what you want, I guess the best I can do is fit you up with a good general work saddle. I got one made up that'd fit you purty good, I think. Medium swells. High cantle. Flat horn. Heavy riggin'. It'll last you twenty years, at least.'

'OK. I'll have to leave that up to you.'

'It's over here on the tree. Climb in it, an' I'll get the stirrups adjusted for you an' see how it fits you.'

An hour later he and Smitty were back

in the buck- board on the way to the ranch. Robert said, 'One thing bothers me.'

'What's that?'

'Why would both Isaac and Sweaty just take my word that I worked for the EV? They handed me a hundred dollars' worth of stuff, and didn't ask for anything.'

'They had your word.'

'So?'

'So they had your word. I 'spect that might be one o' the biggest differences they is betwixt here an' New York City. Most everythin' out here is done on a man's word. There ain't much law and lawyers an' all that stuff. Your word is the most sacred thing you own. If a man's honest, an' does what he says, an' never breaks his word, you kin do most anything in this country. If you ever bust your word, though, ain't nobody'll ever trust you agin. That's why it's fightin' words to call a man a liar. You call a man a liar, you either gotta kill 'im er he'll kill you. An' if anyone ever calls you a liar, you'd best be ready to die provin' you ain't, or fergit about ever makin' a honest livin' again. If you don't learn nothin' else, you best learn right quick to keep your word plumb sacred. You gotta be honest to survive in this country. Either that er jist give up an' be a outlaw.'

Robert was taken aback by the man's vehemence. He made a mental note to comply with that standard. It was going to be a pretty drastic change from life as he had known it.

7

'Hurry up, Runt. Get a move on.'

Robert, or 'Runt' as his name seemed to have been changed to on the ranch, frowned slightly. 'What's the hurry?'

Smitty held up both hands, palms outward. His slow drawl belied the impatient shuffling of his feet. 'Oh, no hurry. Just that time's a-wastin'. The boss don't like us wastin' daylight, that's all.'

Robert moved his legs tentatively. 'I feel stiff as a board.'

Smitty nodded. 'That's natural, that is. You spent half a day on a horse yesterday, an' you ain't used to it yet. Them duds is all brand new, too. Leather chaps, 'specially, is plumb stiff till you get 'em broke in some.'

'So are the boots. I feel like I'm going to fall down when I try to walk.'

'Well, they ain't made fer walkin', that's fer shore. But they's good ridin' boots.

Isaac steered you plumb good. That there's a fine saddle Sweaty sold you too.'

Robert shook his head ruefully. 'It should be. I can't believe how much money I spent, just putting this outfit together. Just so I could hire on. I'm not going to collect any wages at all for three or four months! That saddle alone was a month's wages!'

Smitty bobbed his head in agreement. 'That's a fact. That's a fact. But if you're gonna be a cowpoke, 'stead've a city boy, you gotta have it. It'll likely last you pertneart half o' yore life, though. It ain't somethin' you gotta go out'n buy ever' year, you know.'

Robert moved his head back and forth experimentally. 'This hat makes my head feel like it's top-heavy.'

Smitty chuckled. 'Sorta makes your face smaller'n it used to be, all right. You bein' so little ta start with, it pertneart makes you disappear. If the Injuns come, you kin jist hide right underneath it! You'll be glad you got it, though, when you're spendin' the whole cussed day in the blisterin' sun, come summer. We're a lot closer ta the sun than you was back in New York City. Ain't no trees 'round here, till you gets up in the mountains a ways. Many's the day the only shade you're gonna see is what that hat brim gives ya.'

Robert walked the length of the bunkhouse and back, stepping awkwardly and carefully in his high heeled boots. Smitty hid a grin behind his hand as he watched.

'C'mon,' Smitty said, as Robert completed the lap. 'Let's go.'

'Where we goin'?'

'Oh, down to the corral. The boss has Clint a-pickin' out yore string o' horses. You'll be wantin' to give that new saddle a good test right away, I expect.'

'I rode it for half a day yesterday, remember?'

Smitty coughed slightly. 'Aw, I know that. But that there wasn't your horse. He was jist a plug to get ya a bit used to sittin' in a saddle. He wasn't one o' the string that'll you'll be a-usin'. You'll be wantin' to try it out on your own horse.'

Robert started to say something more, then stopped. He frowned and shook his head slightly, trying to make sense of Smitty's statement. Finally he said, 'Well, let's go look at them.'

He felt conspicuously clumsy as they walked across the yard. He stepped on a rock and turned his ankle, nearly falling. 'Do these heels have to be so high, and slant forward so much?' he complained.

'Oh, you betcha,' Smitty responded at once. 'That's what keeps 'em from a-slippin' through the stirrup an' hangin' you up, if you get throwed.'

'Why would I get thrown?'

Smitty stifled another fit of coughing. He cleared his throat. 'Oh, it happens, time to time. Horse might shy from a snake, er lose his footin' an' fall down, er most anything.'

They approached the corral. Robert noticed a disproportionate number of hands in or around the corral. They all seemed unusually intent on things that didn't seem worthy of their interest. Nobody was looking at him, but the skin crawled on the back of his neck. He felt as if he were being stared at from a dozen directions. He felt suddenly like an over-dressed actor in some Wild West show. It would not have surprised him at all to hear a sudden outburst of laughter and pointing fingers, highlighting his awkwardness.

Smitty opened the gate into the round corral. In the center Clint stood holding the head of a buckskin gelding. Robert's new saddle was already cinched down on the animal. His new bridle was also on the horse, and Clint had a strong grip on it, just above the bit.

The horse's ears were laid back flat against his head. His nostrils were flared. His eyes looked too big for his face. They were rolled clear to one side, watching Robert's approach as though he were some frightening monster. The muscles in Clint's arm were bulged with the effort of holding the horse's head as still as possible. In spite of the obvious effort of holding the horse, Clint was making an admirable effort at appearing casual.

Robert didn't notice. He was admiring the lines of the horse. Even to his unpractised eye, the horse was magnificent. His front legs were thick, corded with muscle. His chest was thick and broad. Layers of muscle bulged beneath the hide. His back was short and straight. His hind quarters were narrow and as corded with muscle as the front legs. His nose was only slightly humped. He had the look of an extremely strong and intelligent animal.

Smitty was speaking. 'This here's Dynamite. He's got the makin's o' one o' the best horses on the spread. 'Course, he might need just a mite o' work, yet. You know, to get 'im to work the way you want 'im to. Everybody wants their horse to work just a mite different, you know. You just hop on up there, an' see what you think of 'im.'

As Robert approached, the animal rolled his eyes more wildly. He kept trying to sidle away, but Clint's iron grip on the bridle kept him from doing anything but moving in a tight circle, edging away from

Robert.

'He acts wild,' Robert observed.

Smitty had another fit of coughing.
'Oh, no. Naw. He ain't wild. He's just one
o' the ranch horses. He just ain't used to
you yet, that's all. All horses sorta tend
to be one-man horses, you know. The
good ones, that is. He'll take to you, right
off. Just hop on, an' run 'im through 'is
paces.'

Robert glanced around. The other
hands had lost all pretense of being busy
about other matters. They had all climbed
the corral fence, and sat perched in a
circle on the top rail, watching.

He stepped up beside the horse. It
continued to try to sidle away from him,
forcing him to try to keep walking, then
lunge as he lifted his unaccustomedly stiff
left leg far enough to reach the stirrup. It
took him three tries before he succeeded.

As he stepped into the saddle, the horse
stopped sidling away. He shuddered. It
felt to Robert as if he crouched, then
stood stock still. Clint kept his grip on
the bridle. Smitty spoke. 'You got both

feet in the stirrups?' he asked.

'Yes.'

'Stirrups adjusted OK, are they? They feel like they fit your legs?'

'Yes, they're fine.'

'You got a good grip on them reins?'

'Of course. Why?'

'You might wanta hang on ta the nub-bin', just a little.'

Robert started to ask 'Why?'

He didn't finish the question. Clint released the horse's bridle and stepped back. Another shudder passed through the horse. He moved his head, tentatively. Then he uttered a squeal Robert had never heard a horse emit before. It sounded almost like a girl whose pigtail had just been pulled by some bully.

Then he learned why the horse was named 'Dynamite'. He exploded. He leaped straight into the air, humping his back so Robert was seated on what seemed like the round top of a moving ball. Then the ball abruptly deflated and dropped from beneath him. The horse's hind legs extended into the air above and to one side of his head, and kicked. The effect of the kick was to make the animal's back snap like a released spring beneath Robert. The horse's front legs hit the ground with bone-jarring force. Robert felt as if the saddle, that had been elusively slipping away from him, was abruptly and permanently implanted in his posterior.

He didn't get time to be concerned about it. The horse removed the saddle as deftly as a surgeon. At the height of the second jump he twisted sideways, spun, dodged, and bucked again. He didn't need to buck again. Before he even gathered himself for that leap, Robert was left dangling in mid-air, flailing wildly. He landed in the dirt of the corral with a thud.

The air was driven from his lungs, and he couldn't force himself to retrieve it. Pain shot through every part of his body. He finally managed to suck in a gulp of air. That hurt too. A cloud of blackness welled up from nowhere and overwhelmed him. In spite of his best efforts, he felt himself being sucked into that black cloud of oblivion. He felt the dirt of the corral against the side of his face. The blackness won, and all sensation left him.

8

Sensation returned to Robert's body slowly. It came in waves of pain, each longer and stronger than the last. He gasped for breath. He was sure he hadn't been unconscious more than a second or two.

He rolled over to his hands and knees. He forced himself to his feet, and staggered a couple steps before he caught his balance. The corral fence, festooned with blurry figures, spun wildly around him.

A chorus of shouts and laughter beat against him.

'Hey, Runt, I thought you said you learned to ride a horse yesterday!'

'Hey, Runt, is that there animal horse enough fer ya?'

'You're s'posed to tuck yer shoulder 'n roll, Runt. You landed like a sack o' flour.'

'That's a fact. I thought the sack was gonna split wide open fer just a minute there!'

The reeling kaleidoscope of color slowed and stopped. Robert sucked in great gulps of air as he looked at the circle of grinning, leering faces perched on the corral.

'Hey, Runt, why don't you tell that there horse how horses act in New York City? Teach 'im not to be so mean.'

Smitty had caught the lunging animal and again had his head held in an iron grip. Robert took another breath, and found he could move with relatively little pain. He looked down at his new clothes. They were smeared with dirt in every spot he could see. A smear of darker brown indicated he had landed where some horse had already been. A rising tide of anger began to swell within him.

A wave of dizziness swept over him, then receded. He took another deep breath. He strode to the horse and climbed back into the saddle. He settled in as solidly as he knew how. He gripped the reins with his left hand, and grabbed the saddle horn with his right. 'Let him go,' he gritted.

Smitty did so, at once. He released the horse and stepped quickly away. The horse squealed again, and leaped high into the air. Again he landed with a shuddering impact and exploded into a second jump.

Robert felt the saddle falling away from beneath him, and fought wildly to pull himself back down into it. He managed to succeed, just as the horse hit the ground again, with sledge hammer impact.

He felt as if his head had been driven downward, clear into his chest. He hung on wildly as the enraged animal leaped again and spun away from him. He lost his grip on the saddle horn. It felt as if some giant hand had simply jerked it away from him. As he sailed through the air, he was vaguely aware he still gripped the reins. He wasn't aware of releasing them as the ground again drove the air from his lungs.

Again, the world receded for an instant, then crashed back with agonizing awareness. He struggled to his feet. Again he was met with the chorus of taunts.

'Hey, Runt, you lasted pertneart two and a half jumps that time.'

'You might make a bronc stomper yet, if you live long enough.'

'Maybe you better quit, Runt. You ain't gonna be able to make it to the dinner table, if you ain't careful.'

'You gotta let your weight down, Runt. He ain't used to nobody sittin' on 'im that's too small to tell they're there.'

Pain radiated through Robert's back and legs. He thought something must surely be broken. He couldn't hurt this much if there were no broken bones. Still, tentative movement gave no evidence of any serious injury. He looked around at the jeering circle again.

He picked up his hat from the dirt of the corral. He brushed at the dirt that covered it, then clamped it tightly on to his head. He strode to the horse Smitty was again holding for him. He wondered, fleetingly, how he had managed to catch the animal so quickly. He stepped into the saddle.

This time Smitty didn't wait for him

to get settled. As soon as his foot hit the off stirrup, he released the animal and stepped away. Dynamite's fuse was perfectly reliable. He exploded on schedule.

In spite of being less prepared, Robert lasted nearly four jumps. Then the dirt of the corral came crashing up to pound the breath from him again.

He rose more slowly. He tried not to listen to the delighted cheering section as he limped back toward the horse. He heard them anyway.

'C'mon Runt ! Tell 'im what yore gonna do to 'im if he don't quit throwin' you.'

'Hey Runt, you better quit while you can.'

'That's more horse than you're ready to ride, Runt. Call it quits.'

As he stepped back into the saddle he was aware of Smitty studying his face carefully. This time he held the horse until he was sure Robert was set. Robert gritted his teeth so tightly his jaw hurt. He nodded his head at Smitty. Again Smitty stepped away. The horse squealed and bucked. Robert fought for breath in the acrid dirt. He couldn't remember losing his seat. He couldn't remember dropping the reins. He couldn't remember anything except the taste of the corral dust, mixed with the acrid metallic taste of his own blood in his mouth.

'Better call it good, Runt. Ain't no sense gettin' yourself killed.'

'You gave it a game try, Runt.'

'That there horse is a mean un, Runt. Best just tell 'im where to go, an' find yourself a good pony.'

Wordlessly, Robert struggled to his feet and staggered back to the horse. He could not keep himself from groaning as he hoisted himself to the saddle.

This time Smitty held on to the horse longer. He spoke softly. 'Listen, Runt. You ain't sittin' right. Get your knees hooked under them swells on your saddle, so you can stay in your seat. Twist your toes out, so's you can hook your spurs in the cinch. An' straighten your legs on the way down enough that your feet in them stirrups'll soak up most o' the jar o' hittin' the ground. Then grip with your legs fer all yer worth. Lean back as far as you can, an' still hold on to that nubbin' real tight. Use it to pull yourself down just as tight into that saddle as you can. An' watch 'is head. You can tell which way he's gonna jump next time by watchin' 'is head. Then you can be ready to lean that way, to keep 'im from duckin' out from under you.'

Robert digested the instructions as quickly as he could. He made the adjustments. He nodded his head. The horse again squealed and exploded into a paroxysm of bucking.

This time, Robert managed to stay with him for more than a dozen jumps. He was even starting to feel a rhythm to the horse's actions, and to anticipate the next surge. Then the horse started to twist one direction. In mid jump, he reversed the direction of the twist, and jerked Robert loose from the firm seat he had in the saddle. The next jump, Robert and horse again parted company.

As he felt himself sailing through the air, Robert rolled his shoulder down and forced himself forward. He hit the ground with the shoulder and rolled, breaking the impact of the fall. He regained his feet to an unexpected round of applause from the corral.

'Way to go, Runt,' somebody called.

Another picked up the attitude change at once. 'You danged near rode 'im that time, Runt!'

'Way to keep at it, Runt,' another called.

'He's got guts. I'll give 'im that,' another conceded to the man perched beside him.

Robert sucked in a great gulp of air and staggered after the determined animal. Smitty actually grinned as he held the horse for him. When he was set, he nodded, and Smitty let the bridle loose.

This time Robert picked up on the animal's rhythm almost at once. He anticipated which jump he would try to reverse directions in mid-jump, and guessed right. The change of direction snapped his neck and sent a stab of pain down the arm holding the saddle horn, but he did not loosen his seat in the saddle.

He thought the horse almost paused when the tactic failed to unseat him. He was sure there was a definite change in the tempo of the bucking. The gelding began to buck almost as if he no longer expected to unseat his rider, but was too stubborn to stop trying.

After another dozen jumps the horse stopped bucking. He stood in the middle of the corral, head hanging, blowing hard. Adrenaline was pumping wildly through Robert's veins. A combination of anger and exhilaration left him feeling like he could never remember feeling before.

He yelled at the horse. 'Don't stop now, you danged idiot! You got so much energy, use it!'

He clapped his spurs to the animal's sides. The gelding squealed, bucked once, then started to run.

Robert had never been on a horse that ran like that gelding. He leaped forward, reaching full speed in three jumps. The side of the corral was already hurtling toward them. Robert instinctively and frantically jerked the reins sideways. The horse responded, spinning at the last possible second. Robert gripped the saddle horn desperately to keep the horse from spinning out from under him.

The horse lunged forward again. Robert felt for a moment that he was going to topple off the animal, straight backward. If he hadn't had a firm grip on the saddle horn, he probably would have. The horse bolted across the corral, and they repeated the previous maneuver at the far side of the enclosure.

After crossing the corral half a dozen times, Robert hauled on the reins to stop him. He responded, coming to a stop in a series of jarring, stiff-legged jumps that again nearly unseated Robert.

Horse and rider were equally exhausted. The horse stood spraddle-legged, unable and unwilling to move. Robert slid from the saddle and staggered, trying with every ounce of determination to keep his feet. He succeeded, but just barely.

An unexpected chorus of cheers erupted from the corral fence. Almost as one man, the hands leaped off the top rail and surrounded him, slapping him on the back and rehashing every jump and fall of his ride.

Robert walked away from the jubilant crew. He limped directly toward Smitty, standing a little way away from the rest. He stopped two feet in front of the cowboy. Smitty met his gaze steadily. An odd light danced in the corners of the old cowboy's eyes, but his face was expressionless.

Robert fought an almost overwhelming urge to plant his fist in the middle of the cowboy's face. He wanted, with every ounce of his being, to smash Smitty's face to a pulp. He swallowed hard and took a deep breath.

Trying to keep his voice as steady as possible, he said, 'Are you satisfied?'

Smitty grinned. He stuck out his hand. 'Hey, Runt, you surprised me. I figgered you'd get stacked up once an' haul off to the bunkhouse in a huff, er sit down an' bawl. You might look like a kid, but you're a better man than I ever figgered you'd be. No hard feelin's?'

Robert hesitated. He did not understand the vicious and dangerous nature of this type of humor. He could have been killed! He could have been seriously injured! Still, nobody else among the crew seemed to think it was anything at all out of the ordinary.

Finally he responded. He reached out and took the extended hand. Smitty's grip was strong and enthusiastic. 'We'll make a cowpoke out o' you, Runt. Mark my words.'

Unseen by the crew, Mack Anderson, owner of the EV, stepped away from the corral. Nodding with satisfaction, he walked across the yard to the house.

'Maybe Frank ain't crazy. The runt just might make a hand after all,' he muttered.

9

Robert gritted his teeth. He would not cry out! He would not groan! He would not give anyone the satisfaction of knowing how severe his pain was. He had no idea he could hurt so much.

He clamped his jaws until the muscles bulged at their hinge. His lips were compressed into a thin line. He swung his feet from the edge of his bunk. Pain shot through his legs, up into his back. It radiated from there down both arms.

He tried to sit up. Pain stabbed through his stomach. He steeled himself against it and forced his body to a sitting position. The pain was so bad it threatened to rob him of consciousness. A wave of nausea welled up, then subsided.

'Hey, Runt,' Smitty called out in his soft drawl. 'You gonna make it this mawnin'?'

'I'm not sure,' Robert groaned. 'At

least I know I'm alive. It couldn't possibly hurt this much to be dead.'

'You might check to be shore. If'n you got anything what don't hurt this mawnin', you might be dead an' jist ain't stopped hurtin' yet.'

'New York City startin' to look better'n it did when you left, Runt?'

'Maybe you could use Dynamite fer a fire horse, Runt. He done a purty good job o' burnin' up the corral with you yestiday.'

'If you'd gain about fifty pounds, he'd at least get tired quicker.'

Several of the hands chuckled at his expense. Robert thought there was a distinct tone of acceptance in their jabs, though.

'Hey, Runt,' Felipe called out. 'I want to see you stand up. I like to see a grown man cry sometimes.'

Another joined in. 'He's a man all right, but he sure ain't grown. Besides, he ain't gonna bawl just standin' up. He's savin' that fer when he climbs back on Dynamite this mornin'.'

Robert felt his face drain of color. He turned to Smitty and spoke softly. 'I don't have to ride that horse again today, do I?'

'If you want 'im fer part o' your string, you do,' Smitty responded. 'You got 'im topped off in great shape yesterday. But he ain't busted, by a long shot. He won't buck near so hard today, most likely, er half as long. But he'll buck again. Fact is, if you bust 'im right, he won't likely ever get to where he won't buck some when you first get on of a mornin'. More just crowhop than buck, to be right honest, but he'll hump 'is back a bit. A horse has to get the kinks out of a mornin' same's the rest of us.'

Robert swallowed hard. 'What if I don't?'

Smitty turned his head to the side, then back. 'Well, then when you do get on 'im, he'll have forgot that he can't throw you, or can't outlast you. You showed him you're the boss. If you let 'im ferget it, you'll just plumb hafta start over. Fer the next week er two, you gotta ride 'im for a little bit, ever' blessed day. You don't

99

have to ride 'im all day, but you gotta ride 'im ever' day. You can't work him a whole lot ever' day. He's jist as tired an' sore as you are. But you gotta ride 'im around the corral at least, ever' day, till he remembers yore the boss. You gotta start teachin' 'im to neck rein, an' to get used to you swingin' a rope off'n 'im. Later you'll have to teach 'im what to do when yore ropin' fer real, but just the rope a-swingin' around'll spook 'im fer a while. Ya gotta teach 'im he don't need to be afraid of it, that you're 'is friend, an' ya ain't gonna hurt 'im.'

Robert groaned inwardly. He couldn't think of anything worse, just now, than climbing on to that horse again. Then he clamped his teeth and headed for the cook house for breakfast. Once he had eaten, he'd ride that animal again or die in the attempt.

As he expected, the rest of the hands were already perched on the corral fence when he got there. Mercifully, Smitty had already roped Dynamite from the remuda and had him tied to the snubbing post in the corral. Robert wasn't sure he could whirl a lariat this morning, let alone throw it far enough to catch a horse.

He hauled his gear out from its spot in the barn and went through the process of saddling and bridling the horse. He mentally ran through a check list of how to put on the saddle, how to tighten the cinch, all the things he had never even heard of a few days ago. He tried to stifle his groan as he picked up the saddle, but was only partly successful. He heard the groan fight its way through his clenched teeth in spite of his best efforts. Pain radiated through his arms, then shot like electricity to every part of his body as he lifted that weight.

Somehow he managed to get the saddle on to Dynamite's back. The horse's hide jerked and quivered. His ears went back flat against his head. His eyes rolled. But he did not make any effort to rid himself of the saddle. 'Savin' that for me,' Robert told himself.

When he had cinched the saddle as tightly as the fire in his muscles would allow him to, he looked at Smitty. Wordlessly the cowboy stepped forward, removed the rope holding the horse to the snubbing post, and held the animal while Robert climbed aboard.

When he was in place he consciously went through the check list in his mind of all the hints Smitty had given him the day before. Knees under the swells. Toes out. Weight in the stirrups. Spurs set in the cinch. Tight grip on the reins. Good grip on the saddle horn. Hat pulled down clear to his eyebrows. He nodded. Smitty released the horse and stood back.

For what seemed like several seconds, Dynamite stood still. Then Robert felt a shudder run through him. Then he exploded.

Robert thought yesterday was bad. It was a picnic compared to the first jump the horse made today. Pain shot through him with fiery intensity. It tore through his buttocks, ripped down his thighs, radiated up his back, and shot down both arms. His neck felt as if his head had been ripped from it. Blackness swept across his eyes. His ears roared.

The horse's hoofs struck the ground with a bone-jarring jolt. As they did, Robert heard a groan escape the horse. His mind raced. 'He grunted! That hurt him as much as it did me! He's sore today too!'

Adrenaline began to course through his system in response to his pain and fear. A sudden burst of elation surprised him. 'I can do this!' his mind shouted. 'Do your best, you four-footed idiot. I'm not letting loose of this nubbin' for anything!'

Almost as if his determination was telegraphed to the animal, Robert could feel the animal's intensity drain away. He jumped three or four more jumps, but there was no fire, no edge of ferocity in them. He just jumped and humped his back a few times, then began to trot around the corral.

The trotting was just as bad as the bucking! Every step shot pain through Robert's battered body. He forced his feet to pick up most of his weight in the stirrups, to stop the unbearable pain to his buttocks. Instantly the pace of the horse hurt less. He began to feel the rhythm of the horse, and to allow his legs to absorb the jar of each step. His body began to move in the saddle to the pace of the rhythm.

The fierce intensity of the pain began to recede. The screaming protest of abused muscles began to abate as those muscles began to warm and limber a little.

A chorus of cheers erupted from the corral fence.

'Look at thet! He's startin' to look like a cowboy in the saddle already!'

'Hey, Runt! You don't ride near so much like a city boy today.'

'He's got balance, the kid does.'

'He's got guts, too.'

'He ain't too big, but he's tougher'n whang leather.'

Soaking in all the praise while studiously pretending to ignore it, Robert rode the horse this way and that around the corral for nearly half an hour. By the end of that time the animal was responding well to the reins. When he stopped the big gelding and slid off his back, the horse even turned his head and bumped him with his nose.

'Looka that!' somebody called. 'Now Dynamite wants to be his friend.'

Robert responded by rubbing the horse's nose briefly, then led him into the barn. He stripped the saddle and bridle off of him, exchanging the bridle for a rope halter. Then he put him in a stall and brought him a can of oats, dumping them into the grain box at one end of the manger. Then he took a curry comb and brushed the horse down well. The horse accepted the attention without objection, munching hungrily on the oats.

Robert's enjoyment of his moment of victory was interrupted by the foreman's voice outside. 'OK everybody! We've had our fun for the day. Now let's get to work.'

Work was the last thing in the world Robert wanted to hear. Work meant being astraddle of a horse. There was no place, no position, no situation that Robert could think of that could be worse just now. 'If it gets any worse than this, I'll just have to tell Sissy she can marry a miner or be an old maid,' he told himself.

Even as the thought went through his mind, he knew it wasn't true. As long as any life coursed through his veins he would do anything in the world to win her hand. Anything. He would succeed at this, or die trying.

Just now he thought the chances were about fifty-fifty.

10

'Here. You'd best strap this on.'

'What is it?'

'Colt forty-five.'

'A pistol?'

Smitty half-smiled. The ignorance of this city boy simply seemed to have no bounds. 'That's what a Colt forty-five is, all right.'

'Why do I need that? I bought a rifle in town, because Isaac told me I needed one. And all those boxes of ammunition. Why do I need another gun?'

'You ain't noticed all the boys wear one?'

'Well, yeah. I've noticed that. It doesn't seem to make sense, though. They all have rifles in their saddle scabbards, the same as I do.'

'Rifle an' a handgun ain't the same.'

'Well I know that. But they both shoot bullets.'

'Purty much where you want 'em to, with that rifle o' yours, I've noticed.'

Robert felt a surge of pride. 'I'd never shot one before. But it wasn't that hard to catch on to. All the things you told me helped a lot. The hardest thing was to keep from flinching. Especially when my shoulder got so sore.'

'You learn quick,' Smitty conceded. 'You still need a hogleg.'

'A what?'

'Hogleg. Handgun.'

'Why?'

Smitty sighed. Why did this green kid have to have a reason for everything? Why couldn't he just take his word that he needed it? 'Well, s'pose yore in a tight, up agin a cut bank, an' yore horse goes down, an' you got a mad cow bearin' down on you. You gonna say, "beggin' your pardon, Mrs Cow. I need to get my rifle outa my scabbard so's I can shoot you?"'

'That doesn't sound like something that's likely to happen. Is it?'

'Oh, maybe not jist like that. But

sit'ations like that come up all the time. Or s'pose yore horse throws you, an' you land 'bout three feet from a side-winder ...'

'What's a sidewinder?'

Smitty sighed again. 'You're shore hard to talk to. You don't know nothin'! A sidewinder's a rattlesnake.'

'There are rattlesnakes out here?'

' 'Course there's rattlers out here. In the summer you don't never put yore boots on, when you're sleepin' out, without tippin' 'em up an' dumpin' 'em. Shake 'em good. Dang things love to crawl inta yore boots of a night. So you get dumped, an' you're three feet from one of 'em, an' he's about to get them fangs inta ya, you gonna ask 'im to wait while ya git yore rifle?'

'That doesn't sound any more likely than the mad cow,' Robert protested.

Smitty sighed again. He looked off across country for a moment. As if reaching a decision, he turned back to the runt of the EV. 'Well, there's always rustlers.'

Robert frowned again. 'Rustlers?'

'Thieves. Fellas stealin' cows. Someone's always a-stealin' the boss's cattle.'

'Who?'

'Well, now if we knowed that, we'd jist go ridin' over an' have us a necktie party. We don't know who! But chances are one of us is gonna ride up on some of 'em one o' these times. If you stumble on to 'em, an' you ain't got a sidearm you kin use, an' use good, you're dead meat.'

'They'd kill me?'

'O' course they'd kill ya! They're rustlers. They'll hang if we know who they are. So if you see 'em, they gotta kill ya er hang.'

'You mean, to stay alive, I'd have to use a gun to kill them first?'

'Well whatd'ya know! He finally caught on. I got this here extra gun an' holster. It's a dandy. It's pertneart as good as my own.'

'Where'd you get it?'

Smitty hesitated a while. 'It belonged to a fella what thought he could outdraw anyone on the face o' the earth,' he explained. 'He was a mite slower'n me.'

'You killed him?'

'Well, I didn't come up dead, so I guess I musta.'

Robert swallowed hard. 'I've heard stories, growing up, about gunmen out west. I thought it was just, just stuff made up. Like legends and stuff.'

'It's a raw country,' Smitty said. 'If you're gonna be part of it, you'd best be learnin' how to stay alive in the process.'

'I don't know the first thing about using a pistol,' Robert protested.

'I figgered as much. You didn't know the first thing 'bout nothin', far's I could tell, when you wandered in here. Now buckle the thing on, an' I'll learn ya how ta use it.'

'You'll teach me?'

'Well, somebody's gotta. If you got one, you'd dang well better know how to use it.'

Robert buckled the gun belt around his waist. 'Now take that leather string at the bottom an' tie it around yore leg,' Smitty instructed. 'Tie it tight enough to keep the holster from a-flappin', an' from pullin' up when ya draw, but don't make it tight enough to cut off the blood in yore leg when you're sittin' a saddle.'

Robert tied the holster down as he was instructed. Then he lifted the pistol out of it. It was surprisingly heavy. 'It's heavier than I thought it'd be,' he observed.

'You'll git used to its weight,' Smitty predicted. 'Now check it to make shore it's loaded.'

Robert turned the gun this way and that, trying to figure out how to open the cylinder. 'Watch where you're pointin' that thing!' Smitty protested. 'Always keep it pointed where it ain't gonna hurt nothin' if it goes off. Even if it's empty.'

'Even if it's empty?'

' 'Specially if it's empty,' Smitty insisted. 'It's the empty gun what always kills someone by accident.'

'How can an empty gun kill someone?'

' 'Cause it ain't always empty when ya think it's empty, ya idiot! When a man thinks his gun's empty, an' goes wavin' it around, an' it ain't acsh'ly empty, that's when it goes off an' kills someone. Always treat a gun like it's loaded an' fixin' to go off, an' that won't never happen to you.'

'I can't figure out how to check it.'

'See that catch right there?'

'Yeah.'

'Pull it back, an' the cylinder'll lay out to the side.'

Robert pulled the catch back and the cylinder opened to the side. 'It's got bullets in it,' he confirmed.

'OK. Now, do you see that whiskey bottle I set up out there?'

Robert looked where the old cowboy was pointing. About seventy feet from them an empty whiskey bottle glistened in the sun. 'Yeah, I see it.'

'OK. Put your gun in your holster. Then when I say "now" I want you to draw your gun an' shoot at that bottle.'

'Uh, all right,' Robert hesitated.

He holstered the gun and waited. When Smitty said, 'Now,' he gripped the handle of the pistol. He pulled it from the holster and lifted it up to arm's length. He sighted down the barrel. He squeezed the trigger. Nothing happened.

'Oh, boy!' Smitty breathed. 'Why do I get myself in these things?'

'What things?' Robert asked.

'Never mind, Runt. Never mind,' Smitty dismissed. 'Here, Let me show you. You say "now" when you want, and I'll show you how it's done.'

'OK,' Robert responded. 'Now.'

The word was scarcely out of his mouth when Smitty's gun barked. The whiskey bottle shattered into a thousand shards scattered on the ground. Robert stared, his mouth agape. 'How did you do that?' he marveled.

'The right way,' Smitty said. 'The way you'd best be learnin'. Now watch an' listen, and I'll show you how it's done.'

He holstered his gun and walked around to the other side of Robert, so his gun was on the same side as the young greenhorn. 'Now, the first thing is how to take ahold o' the gun,' Smitty instructed. 'You got to do two things. You got to git the gun outa the holster, an' you got to cock it. The reason yores wouldn't fire is 'cause you didn't cock it. You got to pull the hammer back. It's a single action.'

'Single action?'

'Yup. Double action'll cock itself when you squeeze the trigger. But you gotta pull too hard to make it do it. You can't hit nothin' thataway. Single action's gotta be cocked afore you kin shoot it, so you gotta pull the hammer back till it clicks. Then it'll shoot.'

He watched Robert until he nodded, then he continued. 'Now, the way you do that is to stick yore thumb on the hammer sideways, like this, afore you draw. Then with yore thumb already on the hammer, you lift it up, only you got to be pullin' the hammer back at the same time you're liftin' the gun. When it's outa the holster, you tip the barrel up to point it at what you're fixin' to shoot at, squeezin' the trigger as it comes up.'

'But the hammer isn't clear back yet,' Robert protested, watching Smitty's hand carefully.

'Keerect!' Smitty agreed. 'That's the trick. When the gun gets up to where it's pointin' at what you wanta shoot, the hammer's back, the trigger's back, an' it's jist yore thumb a-holdin' the hammer. You jist slide yore thumb offa the hammer as it comes level, an' it shoots. Thataway you do it all in one motion.'

'But how do you aim?'

'You don't. This here ain't no rifle.'

'But then how do you hit anything?'

'You point at it.'

'Point at it?'

'Yup. Point your finger at that bottle I shot.'

Scowling in confusion, Robert lifted a hand and pointed his finger at the shattered bottle. 'Is yore finger pointin' at it?'

'Yes.'

'Did you aim it?'

'No.'

'Then how do you know it's pointin' at it?'

'Well, it just is.'

'That's what I'm a-tellin' you. That's how you shoot a pistol. You shoot it an' shoot it an' shoot it, till it's jist like a extension o' yore finger. You practise it, so's you kin do it fast an' smooth, all in one motion. Don't never let yoreself think about where it's gonna shoot. Jist look at what you wanta shoot, an' point at it. Now, here's another bottle. Take it out there where the other one was an' come back.'

'Just one? Shouldn't I take several?'

'I ain't gonna be shootin',' Smitty said with a perfectly straight face. 'I 'spect one'll keep you busy fer long enough. Now git ready.'

Robert did as he was directed, then returned to where Smitty waited. He planted his feet firmly, spread a little apart. He gripped the gun butt, placing his thumb crosswise on the hammer, as Smitty had instructed. He tensed his arm, hunching his shoulder forward, waiting.

'Now,' Smitty said.

Robert jerked the gun from his holster, thumbing the hammer and squeezing the trigger as he did so. The gun barked, kicking up dirt about six feet in front of them.

'Well, at least you didn't shoot yoreself

in the foot,' Smitty observed.

'I wasn't ready for it to go off yet,' Robert protested.

'Then why'd you let yore thumb off'n the hammer?'

'I didn't! I mean, I guess I did, but I didn't mean to.'

Smitty allowed himself the chuckle that had been building up in him. He handed Robert a box of ammunition. 'Here's fifty shells fer it. Shoot 'em all up. One at a time, though. Draw an' shoot, an' try to make it smooth, 'steada tryin' to make it fast. Get used to doin' it. After you're used to doin' it smooth, an' acsh'ly hittin' the bottle, then you kin start workin' on fast.'

'Fifty shells? One at a time?'

'Yup. Then tomorry, I'll be wantin' you to do the same thing. Ever' day, day in an' day out, fifty times. Then when you're in the bunkhouse, an' ya got time on yore hands, take the shells outa yore gun, pick a spot on the wall, and practise. Keep practisin' till you think yore arm's gonna fall off. After while it'll git like second nature to you. The way you take to stuff,

I got a feelin' you might even git good.'

He turned and walked away, leaving Robert to work at getting the hang of the whole thing. When he returned an hour later, the shells were gone. 'I busted three bottles!' he greeted Smitty as he approached.

'Is that a fact? I said I got a feelin' you might git good. I may have to start drinkin' a bit more whiskey, just to keep you in targets. I didn't bust my first bottle till I'd shot up a couple hunert shells. 'Course, I was only ten at the time.'

Robert started to retort, but stopped as Frank, the foreman approached. 'You boys is makin' a lot o' noise out here,' he observed.

'Gonna make a cowpoke outa this runt yet,' Smitty grinned.

'Well, you best leave it for another day,' Frank enjoined. 'We got work to do. Smitty, you take the new kid and check on them cows down south there. Make sure they ain't none of 'em ready to start droppin' calves. Ol' Fred says we got a bad storm a-comin', an' I ain't knowed him to be wrong yet. Make sure they're close enough to the hay stacks to get to feed if the snow gets deep.'

Smitty objected. 'It's pertneart March, Frank. It's felt like Spring fer three weeks. It ain't gonna snow no more this year.'

'Don't kid yourself,' Frank responded. 'I've seen it nice like this early, then drop overnight to thirty below an' dump four feet o' snow in three days. We lost two thirds of our herd in sixty two when it done that. If Fred says we got a change like that a-comin', I don't wanta lose that many cows again.'

The words sounded foreign to Robert. He had never heard of a temperature reaching thirty degrees below zero. He hoped Frank was exaggerating.

He wasn't.

11

'Hey, Runt,' Smitty asked from his bunk, 'what's your real name?'

Robert looked up. He was stationed near the end of the bunkhouse, repeatedly drawing his forty-five, clicking the hammer on the empty casings Smitty had instructed him to put in the chambers, as it came to bear on a spot on the wall. 'Purdy,' he responded.

'No, I mean your whole name. What's your whole name?'

'Robert H. Purdy. Why?'

'What's the H stand for?'

'Hell.'

Everyone in the bunkhouse stopped what they were doing and looked at the diminutive city boy, trying hard to become a cowboy. Smitty sat up, swinging his legs off his bunk. He leaned forward, with his elbows on his knees. 'Hell?' he echoed.

Robert felt his ears redden. He concentrated on his draw with a dogged look. He continued to draw and fire the empty gun, replace it in the holster, then draw again. His brow furrowed with the concentration. He hoped it was apparent that he had no desire to pursue the subject.

The other hand was not at all willing to let the matter drop, however. The sudden blizzard old Fred had predicted had them shut in the bunkhouse. The stove was kept almost red hot against the raging wind and cold. It had been a long and boring day for all of them. They weren't about to let a diversion as promising as this slide by.

'Hell?' Smitty repeated. 'Is that for real?'

Robert nodded curtly, scowling at the wall. He drew and shot the imaginary spot with an imaginary bullet again. 'Yeah, it's for real,' he mumbled.

'Yore folks actually named you Hell?' Smitty insisted.

'My pa did,' Robert acknowledged.

'Why would he do that?' Smitty pursued. 'Was it supposed to be some kind of joke?'

It was apparent the subject wasn't going to get changed or dropped. Robert sighed heavily. He abandoned his practice. He looked around the room. All activity had stopped. Everyone was staring at him, expecting a story. He decided it was easier to accommodate the desire than fight it. Besides, he didn't mind the story as much as he pretended he did. It gave him some measure of notoriety. It was something about him other than his size and his big city background that people could concentrate on.

He sat down and leaned back in his chair. 'Well, no. It wasn't a joke. It was just Pa's way of getting around my ma's religion, I guess. Ma was real strict. Took her religion so serious it was almost a sin to smile. It was worse to say a cuss word, and Pa just couldn't even say "dang it" without her glaring a hole through him. So when I was born, he insisted my middle name be Hell. He was the one that filled out the papers, so that's what he put on my birth certificate.'

'They make out birth certificates when a baby's born in New York?'

'Every one that a doctor or a midwife helps with, anyway.'

'He gived you the name Hell, just so he could say the word around your ma?'

'Something like that I guess,' Robert admitted. 'It worked, too. One time I heard him explain the whole thing to one of our neighbors. I was almost fourteen then, I think. The neighbor asked Pa, "Why in the world would you name your son Hell?"

'Pa, he turned his head and spit a stream of tobacco juice at the sidewalk. That was the other thing he wouldn't let Ma stop him of doing. Chewing tobacco, I mean. He wiped his mouth with the back of his hand, and said, "Well, I thought of it right when the tyke was born. Old Fat Morgan was keeping me company, listening to Ma a-screaming, and he says, 'It's hell giving birth, isn't it?' I just came right back with, 'No, it's Ma

giving birth. It's the kid that'll be hell.'''
That gave him the idea, so when it came
time to name me, Pa insisted that I have
Hell for my middle name. I guess that
means he was the man that really gave
me hell.'

Laughter erupted, rewarding his effort
to utilize the name the way his father had
always done. 'Your Pa actually said that?'
Smitty was incredulous.

'Oh, that's not half of what Pa said,'
Robert insisted. 'He had a whole bunch
of ways he used that name for fun. It's
the only name he ever called me. Mostly
to rile Ma, I suppose.'

'I bet it did, too.'

'Yeah. It came in handy, too, though.
When I hit that age when I was growing
like a weed. ...'

'Now I know you're lyin',' Clint
Hayhorn butted in. 'You didn't never
grow hardly atall, let alone like a weed.'

Laughter erupted in the bunkhouse.
Robert waited till it died down, then responded. 'Well, yeah, I did. I just didn't
keep it up long enough. It was about a

six month affair, then it was all done. Anyway, about that time, I shot up so fast my ma'd add some on to the bottom of my pants, and I'd outgrow them by the time she got them sewed. I can remember always being hungry for a while there. Couldn't get filled up. Ate all the time. Ate the folks out of house an' home. I'd eat supper an' then go after everything left on the table. If you wanted seconds, you'd best be quick. Pa said that was right an' proper, 'cause Hell was supposed to be a bottomless pit.'

Several voices chuckled quietly. Old Fred, the flunkee responded, 'Well, I can see how that'd happen. I raised four boys myself, an' they sure all went through that all right. Funny the name would stick with anyone else, though.'

Robert leaned his chair back and laced the fingers of his hands behind his head. It became obvious that he had decided since the situation was inescapable, he'd just as well milk it for all it was worth. Besides, it sure beat fighting the blizzard to find the cattle and get feed to them.

'Well, it just seemed such a handy thing, having me named Hell. Pa stuck to it till I never thought anything of it. It just plumb got to be my name. He said it was handy in lots o' ways.'

'Like what?'

'Well, I was an active sort, you know. I was always into something. Old Evert Jensen, our neighbor on the first floor, came up to our apartment madder than hobs one day. Said someone had thrown rocks through every one of his windows. Just for fun, it looked like, while they were gone to the store. Right off, Pa's answer was, "Hell you say!"'

'Was it you?'

'Well o' course it was me. Who else would do that? So old Evert answered right back an' says, "Hell, that's what I'm saying all right!"'

'So what happened?'

'Well, Pa just naturally had to pay Evert for the windows. But he made me work to pay it off. He said, "It's Hell to pay that bill." So I done paid it.'

Bufford chuckled, 'Hell, you say!'

Laughter rippled around the room again. Robert nodded. 'That's right. Then Lars Denton came over one day, an' he knew my brother, Rance, was bigger and stouter than most anyone in the neighborhood by that time. He wouldn't ever come out and ask anything directly, though. He'd always try to hint around, like he was afraid to ask a favor. So he came over, an' he said to Pa, "Virgil, who can I go to, to get some help loading that big old piano of mine on to a wagon? I've sold it, but I have to deliver it." An' right off, then, Pa just told him to "Go to Hell". An' Lars bristled up and said, "Hell? He ain't big enough to pull his own pants up." Ma heard him, and come out and says, "Lars, if you're going to talk like that you can leave." So he did, and Pa or Rance neither one had to help him load the piano.'

'He prob'ly thought it was odd to start with, tellin' 'im to go to Hell, when he just asked for a little help,' Bufford observed.

'Oh, he knew who Pa was talking about,' Robert disagreed. 'The neighbors all knew I was Hell. That's all Pa ever called me. He was just peeved 'cause Pa didn't offer Rance to help him.'

'Your pa sounds like a reg'lar joker.'

'He was,' Robert agreed. 'One time I was wearing a shirt that didn't fit so good. It'd gotten tight, you know. It was just too small. Anyway, I stooped over and picked up the axle from a carriage. As soon as my muscles bunched up, the shirt just plumb split right down the back. We went up to the house, an' Pa says to Ma, "Woman, Hell just busted loose."'

'What did she say?'

'Oh, she just kind of smiled and said, "I've been expecting that," and gave me a new shirt she'd sewed.'

'Didn't say nothin' else? Musta got tired o' raggin' your pa about it.'

'I guess.'

Bufford scratched his jaw. 'You know, if your ma was that religious, like you say, you musta had to go to church all the time, livin' in town an' all. I got a sort o' feelin' your pa woulda used that to give the preacher a hard time.'

Robert smiled, admitting to himself that he was enjoying being the center of attention on his own terms. His eyes twinkled. 'Well, I can't deny that did enter in some. They're mostly pretty rigid men, you know. And I have to admit, every time we got a new preacher, Pa sure had fun taking me to Sunday School an' telling him, "Preacher, we came to give you Hell. See if you can straighten Hell out for us."'

'I don't s'pose any of 'em thought it was none too funny.'

'None of them laughed much about it, anyway. Then there was that one day in the middle of a sermon, when the preacher said, "There isn't anything in all creation as bad as hell. Hell is the very worst the mind of God could devise." I was maybe ten, an' I really thought he was talking about me. It made me plumb mad. I stood up right in church an' said, "Preacher, that's not a fit thing for you to say about me."'

'Sorta messed up the sermon some, I'd guess.'

'He did get pretty flustered. He sputtered around about how he was talking about the place, not the boy, but he never did get back on track.'

'And did the congregation think it was funny?'

'Oh, some of them were chuckling a little. Most of the ladies were glaring at us and mumbling about what a diabolical thing it was to give a kid a name like that. After church they just mostly huffed at us, instead of speaking sociably.'

Conversation lagged for a few minutes. All the hands seemed to be reflecting on what a strange name it was, and chuckling softly once in a while. 'I just thought o' somethin',' Bufford interjected.

'What's that?'

'If your folks lived out here, an' they sent you to town in the buck-board, that'd be Hell on high wheels, wouldn't it?'

Robert grinned. 'High red wheels,' he corrected. 'We lived right in the city, remember? But once in a while Pa would hire a carriage for us to go somewhere. He always got one that had the wheels painted red, for just exactly that reason.'

'Did it make you mad, growin' up, that your pa was usin' your name thataway all the time?'

'Not really. I always thought it was funny. In fact, I guess I was about the happiest kid on the block. Pa used that too.'

'How's that?'

'Well, just for example, one Sunday on the way out of church, the preacher asks Pa how we all are, and Pa just told 'im "We're all happy as Hell."'

'Did he ever make the preacher smile?'

'That one? Only once.'

'Your pa actually got 'im to smile with that deal?'

'Yeah, once. He asked Pa once what we was doing for the Lord. Pa told him "Ma and I are just raising Hell."'

The door of the bunkhouse burst open, letting in a flurry of wind, snow and bitter cold. The foreman slammed it shut again, knocking some of the snow off his clothes. 'You boys'd best get a good night's sleep,' he announced. 'Snow seems to be taperin' off some. We'll all be out at first light to try to bust a trail. We gotta get the cows a way to reach the hay stacks. It's turnin' colder, too. Gonna be a bugger by mornin'.'

'Sounds like the day we all been waitin' fer,' Bufford offered.

'Why's that?' the foreman frowned.

'Sounds like the day Hell's gonna freeze,' Bufford responded.

Everybody burst into laughter except the foreman. He just looked around in total confusion. He waited for an explanation, but nobody offered one. He finally shrugged his shoulders and opened the door. Leaning into the wind he fought his way back out into the cold.

12

'One thing about a March blizzard,' Smitty asserted. 'At least you know the snow ain't gonna last too long.'

'It's goin' fast,' Bufford agreed. 'Ain't ary critter in the herd cain't find a dry spot to calve out on.'

Robert nodded through a haze of exhaustion. 'I've never worked that hard in my life,' he moaned.

The two older hands chuckled. 'Calving's hard, all right,' Smitty agreed. 'All them nights with pertneart no sleep. Pullin' calves an' fightin' coyotes an' wolves, an' knowin' ever' time you win you save a cow an' a calf both, that's what makes cowpunchin' worth it.'

'Glad you think so,' Robert argued. 'It's not my idea of fun when I get a calf pulled and save his life and his momma's too, then she turns on me and tries to kill me as soon as she can get up.'

The other two chuckled again. 'It'll grow on ya,' Bufford predicted.

He didn't realize how much it had already grown on him. The raw cold winds of spring faded into the heat of summer. He watched the calves that he had seen struggle to stand. He watched them stagger to the side of the cow to fill their bellies with warm milk. He watched as they began to grow and fill out. He watched them frolic and run, chasing each other in endless circles through the sage brush.

His first branding was an experience he knew he would never forget. It was every bit as much work as calving, but it was a circus of celebration at the same time. Several ranches worked together, rounding up their cattle that were scattered across the range. They sorted and separated, working in endless dust and noise, living with the constant danger of being gored or trampled or caught between thousand pound animals pitted in battle against each other.

One hand from the Circle Cross Ranch

had his horse step in a badger hole. He was running flat out in pursuit of a wayward critter, and never saw the hole. The horse broke its leg and had to be shot. The cowboy broke his neck when he hit the ground. His death cast a pall over the roundup for three days, then faded into the background of the texture of a hard land.

Robert wasn't nearly good enough with a lariat yet to be among those designated as ropers for the brandings. He marveled at the way some cowboy's lariats seemed to be an extension of their arm. They could cast a loop at a running, dodging calf, and almost never miss. If they chose, they could turn the loop over so it opened in front of the animals legs, catching either front or hind legs in its loop instead of the head.

Because he wasn't a roper, he worked days that seemed to never end at the branding fires. He learned to flank calves to throw them from their feet. He learned the techniques of holding either the hind legs or the front, so the others could brand, and castrate almost all the male calves. He held up his end of the work and more, reveling in the occasional word of approval he overheard muttered by one cowboy to another.

As he learned he began to gain the respect of his own crew. Both the respect and the friendship grew, except with Clint Hayhorn. He never missed a chance to make a disparaging comment about Robert, or to try to put him in a spot where he was bound to fail. When he did, he made sure every hand on the place heard about the failure. Then he mocked Robert endlessly for it.

Robert knew he was often the subject of the other cowboys' conversations. The words New York, city boy, and runt just seemed, somehow, to hang in the air. He clearly overheard one grizzled old rancher tell Mack Anderson, owner of the EV, 'That's about the best green hand I ever seen work a brandin'.'

He didn't hear Anderson's response, but he didn't really need to. Others heard the comment as well. It was around the campfire that evening, just after dusk, when Clint's resentment finally boiled over.

Over a steaming cup of coffee, Bufford said, 'Well, Runt, I b'lieve you'll make a hand after all.'

Several of the hands nodded in agreement. Clint snorted. 'Puts on a good show, that's all,' he disagreed. 'I been tryin' all spring to figger out where I seen you afore. Ain't nobody learns that fast. Runt, you ain't no city kid atall. You're that pint-size fella that used to be the bronc wrangler for the Rafter J. He got canned for stealin' from the ranch. You jist pretended to be someone else, an' put on that there city boy act to get hired on. I bet yore real name's Odie Grantham.'

Robert frowned in confusion. 'No it's not,' he protested. 'My name's Robert Purdy. I've never heard of Odie Grantham.'

Clint continued as if Robert hadn't interrupted. 'Came up here an' pretended to be a city boy to get everyone's sympathy. Thataway everyone lets you get by with carryin' half a load, while the rest of us gotta work our selves half to death to pick up the slack. You're a phony, Runt. You're a phony and a liar, and you know it.'

Everyone but Robert realized that Clint wasn't going to back down. They sensed a fight coming, but had mixed emotions. Ordinarily they enjoyed nothing more than a knock-down-drag-out fight to break the monotony of the work. But they liked Robert, and Clint was nearly twice his size. Still they wouldn't interfere. It was a country in which a man had to fight his own fights, and they all knew it.

Robert was still confused by the attack. 'I'll argue with that,' he shot back. 'I pull my weight. I'm a man of my word, and I've done more work the past couple months than I've seen you do.'

'Why you slick-mouthed little runt, you ain't done a day's work since you been here.'

As he talked, Clint stood and walked toward Robert. Robert sat his cup of coffee on the ground and rose warily.

'Yeah, I have,' he responded. 'And I am who I say I am. I don't know what your problem is, but you better go sit down and leave me alone.'

'Oh yeah? And what if I don't?'

'Then I'll have to set you down,' Robert said, as casually as he might have discussed the weather.

There was an instant hush over the roundup camp. Hands from several outfits spotted the fight brewing and hurried for a front row view. Clint's face reddened at the unexpected challenge. His mouth opened and closed twice without sound. Then he charged.

Robert easily sidestepped the charge, sending a short right into Clint's head as he plunged past. The blow felt like a sledge hammer hitting the side of Clint's head. He couldn't believe the runt's fists could be that hard, or hit that fast. The force of the blow, coupled with the unexpected absence of contact with his target, sent him sprawling on the ground.

He sprang to his feet shaking his head, and roared after Robert, swinging wildly.

Elation coursed through Robert's veins. This, at least, he understood.

For several months he had been in a strange world, where he had to learn everything from scratch. He was forced to pit his complete lack of experience against the well-developed skill of seasoned hands, and he knew he usually looked awkward and unsure of himself.

This was something familiar. The streets of New York were as rough and tumble as any cow camp. His father had taught him well. The street gangs had taught him better. He knew every trick, every feint, every ruse in the book. He was deceptively strong in spite of his size. His fists were hardened from a hundred battles, and he had learned to hold his own against men that always seemed to be nearly twice his size.

He stepped outside Clint's wild roundhouse right and delivered two hard chops, one to Clint's midsection and one to his chin. Blood flew from a cut the blow opened on his chin. Then he ducked away before the cowboy could respond or counterpunch. Clint grunted with each blow and hesitated, then charged again.

Robert sidestepped again, smashing a blow into Clint's ear as he passed.

Clint kept his feet that time and whirled to charge again. Robert met him with a straight right to the chin that opened another cut. It stopped him in his tracks for an instant. Before he could shake off the blow and continue the charge, Robert was no longer in front of him.

Robert moved around him in a circle, jabbing, chopping, pounding away on the bigger man without ever giving him the opportunity to use his size and weight. Almost every time Robert's fist connected with his face or head, the skin tore and blood began to flow. Clint began to slow noticeably.

After another charge that resulted in three more ringing blows to his head, Clint dropped his arms. He leaned forward, as if he was going to drop to his knees. Then he suddenly dived for Robert's legs.

It was far too old a trick to catch

Robert off guard. Instead of backing away, however, he stepped forward and lifted his knee as hard as he could into the diving cowboy's face. Bone crunched and blood flew as it contacted.

He sidestepped and watched the cowboy collapse on to the ground. He started to send a booted foot into the man's ribs, then hesitated. Clint did not move.

Trying hard to appear that he was not even breathing hard, Robert walked back over to his coffee and sat down, crosslegged on the ground. There was not a mark on him. The blood that smeared his hands and clothes was all Clint's.

As he sipped his coffee, the dam of silence broke. That silence had dropped on to the camp when Clint dived for his legs. A collective gasp marked the contact of Robert's knee with his adversary's face. Then it seemed as if every cowboy watching held his breath to see if Robert would continue to punish the beaten man when he was down. Now their voices raised in cheers and congratulations.

'I guess he picked on the wrong man

that time!'

'For a runt, you pack quite a punch.'

'Boy, you sure did a job on him, Runt.'

'I ain't never seen a man fight that good in my life!'

'He wiped up the camp with him, an' he ain't even breathin' hard.'

'Did you see that? He went over an' sat down an' went to finishin' his coffee! Like he just put it down to swat a fly er somethin'.'

Frank strode into the gaggle of comments. His voice rose above the rabble. 'All right boys. You've had your entertainment for the evenin'. Now you'd best all get turned in. I want every hand in the saddle by sunup.'

The grouped cowboys began to disperse, walking to their bed-rolls. Frank called out to the roundup cook, 'Dick, you'd best see to Hayhorn. Make sure he's OK. Then send someone to babysit 'im back to the ranch. He ain't gonna be any good on roundup for a few days. Ol' Fred'll tend to him till he's up an' around again. Runt, you'll be needin' to pick up his share o' the load. You disable one o' my hands durin' brandin', yore the one that'll be doin' double work.'

The cook strode to the still down cowboy and began tending to him. As Robert drifted off to sleep he was vaguely aware of a couple hands helping Clint on to his horse. Then he and another man rode slowly out of camp.

He slipped into a deep slumber with a smile playing around the corners of his mouth.

13

'Another bunch missin'?'

Frank nodded glumly. 'Fourth bunch this month,' he answered. 'Not big bunches. Eight er ten at a time. Big steers mostly.'

The cook house was crowded with every hand that worked for the Eden Valley Cattle Company.

'You know good'n well who's doin' it,' Bufford offered.

'How do you figger that?' Mack Anderson demanded.

'Plain as day,' Bufford insisted. 'First, Clint goes an' picks a fight with the runt. Then Runt whupped up on 'im so good he couldn't get outa bed fer four days. Then he lit a shuck jist afore we all got back from roundup. It wasn't more'n a month after that we started missin' them little bunches o' cattle.'

'If it is Hayhorn,' Anderson argued,

'why did he wait a month before he started?'

When it was obvious Bufford didn't have an answer, Smitty offered one.

'Well, he wasn't up to snuff when he left, fer one thing. He was still nursin' some mighty sore ribs an' a busted nose, among other things. An' if he was fixin' to get even with Runt by stealin' from you, he'd have to have somethin' to do with 'em once he stole 'em. That'd all take about a month, seems to me like.'

Silence reigned while everyone considered the logic. Nobody could fault it, so they all finally just looked at the boss, waiting for him to make some sort of decision.

Anderson sighed. 'Well, we ain't gonna solve it sittin' around here. You all be on the lookout real sharp. Keep your guns oiled an' ready. I'll give three months' wages to any hand that catches 'em red-handed. Just don't go gettin' yourselves killed.'

'You got any idea where they're takin' 'em?' a hand asked.

'Not yet. Hope to in a few days. Smitty and Light Horse are gonna trail that last bunch. It rained a couple days ahead of when they took 'em, so Light Horse probably can.'

Somebody snorted. 'That half-breed Shoshone can track a jackrabbit on bare rock in a windstorm.'

A murmur of agreement rippled around the room. Light Horse gave no indication he even heard.

'Well, if that's all anybody's got to say, Frank'll give you your orders for the day,' Anderson said.

It was a full week later when Smitty and Light Horse rode back into the ranch yard. It was after suppertime, but the cookhouse soon filled with every hand on the place. The returning pair scarcely had time to eat a late supper when Anderson and Frank strode in. 'What did you find, boys?' Anderson asked without preamble.

'Well, it's like Lester said,' Smitty offered. 'Light Horse kin track a jackrabbit. They was plumb hard to track, though.

Hid their trail sometimes, mixed it into the main road when they could.'

'So where did it lead?' Anderson demanded.

'Rock Springs.'

Silence suspended the room for a moment. Then Anderson asked, 'You track 'em clear into town?'

'Nope. Five miles out, er so.'

'You go on into town?'

'Nope. We figgered we'd best not tip our hand. Leastways, not till we reported back, an' you told us what to do.'

'Then you don't know what they're doing with them once they get there?'

'No idea.'

Silence gripped the room again. Uncomfortable at speaking out, Robert decided it was imperative. 'Uh, I have an idea.'

'What's that?'

'I lived in Rock Springs a while when I first came out here. Meat's pretty hard to come by in Rock Springs sometimes. Too many miners and such, for a small town to deal with. There are people selling beef and venison and even buffalo once in a while out of the back of wagons. They sell it to stores or cafes or boarding houses, or just to people.'

'You think they're sellin' our beef on the street?'

'That'd be my guess,' Robert reiterated.

Silence descended again as everyone chewed on the thought. Anderson said, 'Well, that'd answer how they get around our brand bein' on 'em. How we gonna find out? Any ideas?'

At the first mention of Rock Springs, Robert's heart leaped into his throat. His loneliness for Sissy had become increasingly unbearable over the past months. Mention of Rock Springs had pushed it way beyond his tolerance level. Then an idea flashed into his mind. He couldn't think of anything wrong with it, so he spoke again.

'Uh, I know Rock Springs pretty well. I still have all my old clothes. I could go back there and look and act like a miner till I find out if they're selling it there, where they're holding them until they butcher, and all that. Then I could either come back and let you know, or get word over to Green River, to Sheriff Young.'

Silence bounced around the room for another long moment. 'Anybody got a better idea?' Anderson asked.

Nobody responded.

He turned his attention to Robert. 'You got any special reason for volunteerin'?'

'Yes sir.'

'What?'

'I have a girl waiting for me there.'

'You got a girl in Rock Springs?'

'Yes sir. Her name's Narcissa Spaulding. Her pa owns the Mercantile Store. We're planning on getting married when we get situated so we can homestead.'

The hands of the EV looked at each other in stunned silence. It was Smitty that finally said, 'Runt, you got a girl yore thet sweet on all this time, an' you ain't even mentioned her?'

Robert shrugged. 'I don't miss her quite as much if I don't talk about her. I can't help thinking about her all the time, though.'

'So how do I know you ain't gonna just think about romancin' that girl and forget about what I'm sending you there to do?' Anderson demanded.

Robert's answer was simple, quiet, and firm. 'My word.'

Anderson nodded. 'Good enough for me. Ride out at sunup.'

He probably should have waited for sunup. He just couldn't. An hour before sunup Robert was in the saddle. He nudged his horse to a ground-eating trot. His heart hammered in his chest. He willed the horse to move faster. It was only with a gargantuan effort that he made himself stop regularly to rest the animal, to let him drink from small streams and puddles, to not push him too hard, too fast.

It took from before sunup until after dark to get to Rock Springs, riding as hard as his horse could tolerate. When he entered town, he rode directly to Spaulding's Mercantile Store, tied his horse to the hitch rail and stepped up on the sidewalk. He pulled his hat down so his face was shaded, and stepped through the door.

Sissy Spaulding put down a stack of dry goods and turned toward him. 'Can I help you?' she asked. 'We were just getting ready to close.'

'You could give me a kiss,' Robert responded.

Sissy gasped and took a step backward. Her face flushed with anger. 'Why, I ....' she started to huff.

Robert swept his hat off, grinning from ear to ear. Sissy gasped again. Her hand flew to her mouth. A tiny whimpering squeal escaped between her fingers. Then she found her voice. 'Robert!' she cried, opening her arms and lunging toward him.

He took her in his arms and whirled her in a circle before letting her feet touch the floor again. Then she decided his original request wasn't out of line after all. She complied eagerly.

She stepped back, keeping her hands on Robert's arms. 'Oh, Robert, I've missed you so much! It's been so long!

I have all your letters. All four of them. And you look so, so different. You look like a, a cowboy!'

'You want a cowboy, you got a cowboy,' he responded.

They stared at each other, drinking in each other's presence as if they had been dying for the thirst of it. It was Narcissa who spoke next. 'How did you manage to make it into town?'

'On business,' he said.

A shadow passed across her eyes. 'Business?'

He nodded. 'Somebody's been stealin' our beef.'

'Our?'

'EV beef. The ranch. There's a half-breed Indian that's one of the hands. He and another cowboy tracked them almost to Rock Springs, so we think they're bringing them here and butchering them to sell the meat. The boss sent me to find out.'

'Sent you?'

'Well, I sort of volunteered. I said I could pretend to be a miner, and nobody'd pay any attention to me. That way I can nose around, look for the man I know that's probably behind it, and find out where they're holding and butchering them. Then we can catch them red-handed with some of our cattle, and put a stop to it.'

'But that sounds dangerous.'

He shrugged. 'I suppose it is. I'll be careful.'

'Will you be staying at the boarding house?'

'I suppose I'd better. I'd rather stay at your place.'

'But we don't have an extra bedroom.'

'So much the better.'

She cuffed him playfully. 'Robert Purdy! I'll wash your mouth out with soap!'

'You're plumb welcome to try.'

'Plumb welcome? You're even starting to talk like a cowboy.'

'Why, shucks, Ma'am, 'tain't nothin' to thet thar.'

She giggled and came into his arms again. He suddenly hoped it was going to take a long while to catch these rustlers.

14

Good luck can be a curse. Robert hoped it would take at least a couple weeks to ferret out the purveyors of EV beef in Rock Springs. As luck would have it, it took a couple days.

When he could tear himself away from Narcissa at the store, he stabled his horse in the barn behind the Spaulding house, along with their milk cow. He rubbed him down well and gave him a generous feed of both hay and oats. Then he changed clothes, leaving all of what had become his normal clothes and equipment in the Spaulding house. He put on the clothes he had worn before going to the EV Ranch. They felt soft and strange to him.

It surprised him that he felt completely naked and vulnerable without the forty-five at his hip. He tried to figure out ways he could wear it beneath his clothes, but knew he could not, without its obvious presence betraying him.

Then he went to Swenson's Boarding House. 'Are you back again?' Mrs Swenson greeted him. 'I thought you were long gone from here.'

'You can't get rid of a bad penny,' Robert grinned. 'My old room empty?'

'Well, by chance it is. Well, not by chance. You can find a room most anyplace in Rock Springs, if you're white,' she bemoaned.

'Why's that?'

'More and more Chinese in the mines,' she sighed. 'The U.P. is getting worse and worse. You'll notice at the supper table. You will be taking your meals here again?'

'Sure thing,' he assured her.

'You have money?'

'Sure thing,' he repeated. 'Price the same?'

'Same,' she echoed. 'Week at a time in advance. Not that I'd worry about you paying.'

She was right about the supper

conversation. The vehemence of every miner's hatred of the Chinese bothered him greatly.

'Gave me and Henry a room to work, with a decent seam o' coal,' one of them growled, 'then took it away again. Them rat-eatin' pagans claimed he'd given them that room to work the day before. They weren't workin' it at all, so the straw boss give it to us. It was a good room too. We coulda made good money for a week or two. But since them disciples o' Confuse-us bellyached about it, he moved us down the entry a ways an' give us a room we couldn't hardly get no coal outa at all. Just an' old seam that was plumb wore out already.'

'Somebody oughta get rid of all of 'em,' another miner agreed. 'An' the sooner the better.'

'Killin's too good for them heathen,' another chimed in. 'Oughta go over there to Hong Kong an' burn 'em out. With luck we could burn up half of 'em along with that town they got built up across the crick there.'

The conversation throughout supper stayed in the same vein. There was even talk of a way it could be done. Hong Kong, as it was called, was the Chinese section of Rock Springs. It was separated from the rest of the town by Bitter Creek. Two bridges spanned the gully with its small stream of water. The first speaker opined that if the bridges were blocked, the Chinese would have no way to run from an organized group of white miners. They could 'clean out that rat-nest,' he declared.

Robert found himself avoiding meals at Swenson's. Partially he hated the vein of the constant heated vitriol against the Chinese. More than that, he used every excuse he could find to eat at the Spauldings' instead.

As he left the Boarding House the third day in town he spotted Clint Hayhorn. He stopped dead in his tracks, looking for someplace to duck out of sight. Then he remembered how different he looked in his 'New York outfit'. His soft cap with its leather bill effectively concealed much

160

of his face. Everything else about him, except for his size, looked so different he wasn't sure he would recognize himself.

Buoyed by the conviction that he was effectively disguised, he approached. The former EV hand was selling something from the back of a wagon. He saw at once it was freshly slaughtered beef. The meat was still steaming slightly in the early morning air.

He eased back into the shadows of a building and watched. It took the cowboy less than an hour to sell all the meat he had with him. Then he hopped back up on the seat of the wagon and turned his team down the street. Robert followed on foot, trying to stay out of sight.

Hayhorn led him out of Rock Springs to the north. Less than half a mile from the edge of town, the wagon disappeared down into a draw.

Moving stealthily, Robert worked his way through the sage brush to the lip of the rim. He peered carefully over the edge.

In the bottom of the wide gulley, less

than a quarter of mile from his vantage point, a makeshift corral had been erected. Within it a dozen head of cattle bore the easily readable EV brand.

A block and tackle was fastened to a large, stout limb of a cottonwood tree. From the bottom pulley a rope reached out across the ends of a three-foot piece of post. Both ends of the rope were secured to a meat hook. Beneath the arrangement the ground was littered with pieces of hide, meat and bone. The dirt was black with dried blood. Flies swarmed over it all.

'Butchering them right there,' Robert breathed. 'One a day, I bet. Maybe two. Then they haul it into town and sell it.'

Five bed-rolls were laid out on the ground a ways beyond the corral. Remains of a small fire trailed a thin tendril of smoke near the bed-rolls.

The five men were each taking their share of the money Clint was doling out. Then they sat down and started a game of cards. Robert backed slowly and carefully away from the edge of the draw and trotted back to town.

Thoughts tumbled across each other in his mind. Green River was twelve miles away. The sheriff may or may not be there. If he were there, he may or may not be interested in Robert's story. By the time he could get the sheriff there, the five men may well be gone to raid the EV herd again.

He also remembered clearly the words of Mack Anderson. 'Three months extra wages to catch them red-handed,' Robert breathed. 'That'd sure come in handy. That much closer to being able to get married. I don't know if I can stand to go back and leave Sissy here again.'

The idea of riding back to the ranch with his information crossed his mind. That was an awfully long day's hard riding each direction. That made two days at the very least before he could bring the crew back. With the whole crew, it would take an extra day. Who knew where Hayhorn and company would be by then?

By the time he got back to the

163

Spauldings', his mind was made up. He changed back into what had become his normal clothes. He retrieved his horse, rested and ready. He checked both his forty-five and his forty-four-forty carbine. Then he stopped by the Mercantile Store to let Sissy know what he was going to do.

She was not pleased. 'You're going to do what?'

'I'm going to go out and arrest Hayhorn and his sidekicks.'

'By yourself?'

'Why not?'

'Because there are five of them! You'll be killed!'

He shook his head. 'I can handle myself. I can walk right up to them without them even seeing me. They're not watching for somebody to catch them at all. I'll have my rifle. They won't try anything when I've already got the drop on them.'

She was not convinced, but she could think of nothing to change his mind. 'But if they do give up, what will you do with them?'

'Bring them back here.' His words

indicated he had already thought it through. 'We can lock them in that store-room. There's no way out of there. Then I'll ride over to Green River and get the sheriff.'

She opened her mouth several times, but no ready arguments availed themselves. 'I'll be back in an hour,' he promised. 'Have the storeroom ready.'

Before she could protest he was out the door and gone. A sob broke through her lips as she watched him disappear, his horse moving at a swift trot down the street.

Instead of riding to the spot from which he had spied on the rustlers, Robert rode a wide circle around, approaching the camp from the opposite side. He had spotted what he thought would be the perfect place from which to accost them.

When he was as close as he thought he could ride unheard, he dismounted. Pulling his rifle from its scabbard, he checked the chamber to be sure it was fully loaded. Then he moved quietly to a cluster of rocks at the rim of the draw.

Slipping silently through the boulders, he moved to a spot that gave him an unobstructed view of the camp. The five men were still sitting in a circle playing cards. Money was scattered in front of each of them, and in the center of a blanket they had spread on the ground.

Robert squatted behind a boulder, resting his rifle on the top of the rock. Then he called out, 'All of you put up your hands! You're under arrest!'

The response was anything except what he had expected. At the first word from his mouth, the five men moved as if released from springs. They scattered, diving behind clumps of brush and rocks. By the time he finished his well-rehearsed speech, bullets were ricocheting off of the rocks around him.

From his vantage point he could see two of the rustlers, lying prone in the grass, behind too-small clumps of brush. Aiming carefully, he squeezed off a shot, and was rewarded with the 'thunk' of a bullet striking flesh. The man he had shot at jerked once and lay still.

Rock fragments showering his face and head, he took aim at the second man he could see and fired again. The man leaped up, then fell back down and lay without moving.

The barrage of fire directed at him suddenly stopped. He could hear the scurrying of swift and frenzied movements, but could see nothing. Then he heard hoof-beats galloping away.

He sighed and stood up. He swore softly. 'Now who'd have thought they'd do that?' he muttered to himself.

He looked back at the two prone figures on the ground. He sighed again. Holding his rifle loosely, he made his way back to his horse. He slid the rifle into its scabbard. He lifted his foot to the stirrup.

'You must be the city boy.'

The words sent an icy jolt down his spine. He put his foot back on the ground and turned slowly. Less than twenty feet away stood one of the men who had been playing cards. 'I, I thought you rode off,' he said.

The man laughed shortly. 'Thought

you might think so. Clint an' Lew did. I thought I'd stick around and wait till you put that rifle up. You're a mite too handy with it.'

Realizing suddenly he had nothing to lose, that the man intended to kill him, Robert said, 'You're under arrest for rustling. Drop your gunbelt. I'm taking you back to town.'

The man laughed that short, hard laugh again. 'In your dreams, city boy. You're about to learn how we deal with city boys out here. Just like in them dime novels. I'm gonna count to three, an' when I say three, I'm gonna kill you.'

Robert's heart pounded in his ears. He fought to take in a breath. He was almost sure he had removed the loop of leather from his gun's hammer before he took up his position in the rocks, but he wasn't positive. Now there was no way to check. Even if he had, he had never in his life drawn his gun against another person. He had practised endless hours. Smitty had assured him he was as fast as anyone he'd ever seen. That was suddenly no comfort at all.

'One.'

He considered offering to let the man ride away, scot free. Maybe he would take the offer instead of taking the chance he was faster.

'Two.'

He saw the tensed posture of the outlaw. His fingers were curled, less than two inches from the butt of his gun.

'Three!'

The word wasn't out of the rustler's mouth before his hand closed on his gun butt. His thumb was pulling the hammer back even before the barrel cleared the holster.

Robert's mind was in turmoil. He couldn't think. He couldn't still the hammering of his heart. He could only react. Exactly as he had a thousand times in practice, his hand made the move to grip his gun, to thumb the hammer, to squeeze the trigger, to point without thinking or aiming, to slide the thumb off the hammer.

The gun in his hand bucked. He heard

two shots almost at the same time. An angry whine whipped past his left ear. The outlaw grunted and took a step backward. The gun in Robert's hand bucked and barked again, as if of its own accord. The rustler grunted again, and took another step back. A third time, all in less than two heartbeats, Robert's gun spoke. The would-be killer fell backward, his forgotten gun still gripped in dead fingers.

Robert swallowed hard. He stood, holding the gun. A thin tendril of smoke wafted from the barrel. A tremor passed through his body. He swallowed again. He holstered his gun. He was startled by the sound of choked sobs. It took several seconds to realize they came from his own lips.

15

'I didn't even have to stomp on anyone's toe.'

Sissy frowned. 'What?'

He chuckled. 'I just thought about something that happened a long time ago. Back in New York. A guy by the name of Rick Donavan wanted to beat me up something awful. He just couldn't do it, and he knew it. So one day he slipped up behind me and grabbed me around the arms, so I couldn't defend myself. Then he had two of his friends that were going to beat me up while he held me.'

'Oh, dear! What did you do?'

'The only thing I could think of. I don't remember who told me about it, but it worked. I just stomped on his toe as hard as I could. It surprised him enough he relaxed his grip on my arms. Then I just went limp and dropped right out of his grip. One of the others was just swinging at my face, and when I wasn't there, he hit Donavan instead.'

She giggled. 'I bet he was surprised.'

'It wasn't exactly how he thought things would work,' he agreed. 'Anyway, I got in a few pretty good licks, then got away from them before they could grab me again.'

'Why on earth did you think of that now?'

'I'm not sure. I guess because it was the only other time I was by myself against several other guys. Then I'd have just gotten beat up though. Donavan wasn't a killer. This time, I thought I was going to get killed.'

'You could have, too,' she scolded. 'I tried to get you to go after the sheriff.'

'I still don't think I'd have had time.'

Sissy glared at him. Her fear had been translated into anger with him, so that she could handle the emotional turmoil. She was still afraid to release the anger, lest she go to pieces. 'You could at least talk to the deputy here in Rock Springs.'

'I didn't know there was a deputy here.'

Tears brimmed suddenly in Sissy's eyes. The anger seemed to melt from them. 'I should have told you. I was just too upset about your going after those men alone. Oh, Robert, I was just sure I was going to lose you.'

A sob broke through her composure. He held out his arms and she rushed into their comforting circle. He held her close, smelling the perfume in her hair, feeling her body pressed against him. He thought he could just stand there all day, if she wanted.

She pulled away much too soon for his liking. 'You need to go talk to him, though.'

'I suppose that'd be best. Where would I find him?'

'He has an office a block over, but he's not usually there. There might be a note on the door saying where he is, though.'

Robert nodded. 'I'll be back.'

He walked out of the store and stepped into the saddle. He nudged his horse, reining him around, heading for the deputy sheriff's office. As luck would have it, he was there.

'Excuse me. Are you the deputy?'

The angular old man eyed him with amusement lurking in the corners of his eyes. 'Well now, that's usually what the badge means. What can I do for you?'

'Uh, oh. Sorry. I didn't see the badge. The way you were standing, I mean.'

'The name's Ike Woods. So what can I do for you?' the deputy repeated.

'Uh, my name's Robert Purdy. I ride for the EV.'

'Figgered that from the brand on your horse.'

Robert took a deep breath. 'The boss sent me down here to see if I could find out who's been stealin' our beef, and what they're doing with it. I saw a fellow that used to work for the EV selling fresh beef, so I followed him back to his camp. He and four other men had a corral built there, with EV beef in it. They were butchering it and selling it in town.'

'That so? Butcherin's hard work. Hard work an' stealin' don't gen'ly go together.

So I 'spect yore wantin' me to run out there an' arrest these five, huh?'

'Uh, no sir.'

Wood's eyebrows shot up. 'No?'

'No. Like I said, I followed them. I found a spot in the rocks above their camp where I was pretty well protected, and pointed my rifle at them, and ordered them to put up their hands. I, uh, I thought I could arrest them. I didn't know there was a deputy here. I thought by the time I rode over to Green River and back, they'd probably be gone.'

'You threw down on five cattle rustlers, all by yourself? An' yore standin' here tellin' me about it? What happened?'

'Well, instead of surrendering, they scattered and started shooting at me. I shot two of them. Then I heard horses running away, and I thought the rest got away, so I went back to my horse. Just after I put my rifle back in the scabbard, one of them that hadn't run forced me to draw against him. I shot him too.'

'Where you from, son?'

'New York.'

'New York City?'

'Yes sir.'

'How long you been out here, Boy?'

'Almost a year. I tried mining for a little while, but I didn't like it. Then I hired on at the EV, and have been learning to be a cowpoke. Anyway, I knew people here in town, so Mr Anderson asked me to come down and see if this was where his cattle were being taken.'

'Who do you know in town?'

'Well, the Spauldings, mainly. We, I mean, uh, Narcissa and I intend to be married.'

'Ah! So you're that little runt from the big city that she went an' flipped head over heels over. I heard about you. Now you went an' kilt some fellas.'

'Yes sir.'

'So you're turnin' yourself in?'

Robert frowned. 'No! I don't believe I've done anything wrong. I simply tried to arrest some thieves, and then I was forced to defend myself. I wanted you to come out and see what the situation is, so somebody won't try to lodge charges against me.'

'From the city all right,' Woods muttered. 'Ain't heard nobody talk that fancy outside o' the lawyers over on front street. All right. Show me.'

Retrieving his horse, the deputy mounted. Riding side by side, they trotted to the draw north of town. The deputy sat his saddle, turning this way and that, sizing up the situation. He dismounted and walked to where the block and tackle was rigged to the tree. He grabbed a wadded hide and spread it out. 'EV, all right,' he confirmed. 'Just like all of 'em in the corral.'

'The other one is up there,' Robert pointed.

The deputy reined his horse around and let him pick his way up the far side of the draw. At the top the rustler lay where he had fallen. His gun was still on the ground, inches from his hand. 'He made you draw, you say?'

Robert nodded. 'He said he was going to make me die just like they did in the dime novels. He counted to three, and we were supposed to draw when he said "three". He was already drawing when he said it, though.'

'And you beat 'im anyway.'

'Yes sir, I guess I did.'

'You ever draw against a man afore?'

'No sir.'

'You know who that man is?'

'No sir.'

'His name's Joe Tyne. Small time thief and big time gunman. He's kilt four er five fellas that I know of. Always makes 'em draw agin' 'im, an' always out-draws 'em. Fast man with a gun. You must be almighty fast, if you beat 'im. Are you almighty fast with that gun o' yores?'

'I, I don't really have any idea.'

'Who teached you how?'

'Smitty. Drew Smith, I guess his name is. He just goes by Smitty. He gave me the gun and taught me to use it.'

'That explains it. Smitty's greased lightnin' with a gun. Can you beat 'im?'

'Smitty? Yeah. I couldn't at first, but after while I got to where I could beat him pretty easy. Why?'

'Well, that 'splains why Tyne didn't have a chance agin ya. I 'spect you'd best git these critters herded back to the EV. Dozen head still in the c'ral, looks like. I'll get the undertaker ta take care o' these boys. I'll file a report with the sheriff, so there won't be nobody bringin' charges against ya. Purty clear cut situation, looks to me like.'

'Thank you. I'll go back into town and get my things, then get started right away.'

It took longer than he wanted to gather his things and say goodbye to Sissy. The goodbye was the hard part. He promised her that he would find a way to get to town at least every two months to see her, and they would find a way to wed within another year. It wasn't even close to what either one of them wanted, but it seemed the best he could do.

16

It took four days. Each seemed a year long to Robert. Twelve head of cows were easy enough to herd along. He wanted them in good shape when they reached the EV, though. He wanted more than anything, just now, for both Mack Anderson and the foreman, Frank Ritter, to be impressed with his exposing of the cattle thieves, breaking up their operation, and bringing back at least some of the stolen cattle. For that reason, he had to let them have time to graze, to lay down and chew their cud, to drink, and to rest.

Without the cattle, he could have made the ride in one long, hard day, knowing his horse would have time to rest up afterward. The first night out was the hardest. It was almost more than he could do to keep from leaving the cattle, once they were bedded down. He argued with himself that he could ride swiftly back to

Rock Springs while they were bedded, see Sissy for a while, then be back before the cattle stirred. 'Just my luck a pack of wolves would show up if I did,' he muttered as he spread out his own bedroll.

The sun was drifting down behind the mountains when he hazed the small herd into the ranch yard the fourth night out. Hands emerged from all directions, it seemed to Robert, to greet him.

'Hey, Runt. Where'd you find the cows?'

'Did you find the rustlers?'

'You know who's doin' it?'

'Yore sweetheart still waitin' fer ya, er did she run off with some miner?'

'I opened the gate to the big corral, Runt. Run 'em in there till mornin'. Then Frank'll figger out what to do with 'em.'

'They look in purty good shape, Runt. Must be turnin' into a cowpoke fer real.'

Robert grinned at the reception. He felt as if he had come home. Even missing Sissy couldn't steal the warm feeling of belonging.

As he turned his horse back from

corralling the cattle, Frank was waiting. He stepped off his horse as the foreman approached. 'Good to see you back,' Frank said. 'You find 'em?'

Robert nodded. 'I found them. They were taking them to Rock Springs. They had a corral set up north of town. They were butchering one or two a day and selling the meat on the street.'

'They?'

'Clint Hayhorn and four other men.'

Frank nodded. 'Figgered him fer one of 'em. Who's the others?'

Robert shrugged. 'I didn't know any of them. One of them was named Joe Tyne.'

Frank grunted. 'I know 'im. Whatd'd ya do?'

'I tried to arrest them. They started shooting instead. I killed two of them. Then the rest got to their horses and took off. Or so I thought. Then Tyne showed up at my horse, and I had to draw against him.'

'You drew against Joe Tyne?'

'Yeah. I had to. He didn't leave me any choice.'

'And beat him? Well, I guess that's a stupid question. Course ya beat 'im, er ya wouldn't be standin' here.'

Robert didn't answer. After a long pause Frank said, 'Well, whatd'ya know? Well, git yore horse took care of. Supper's pertneart ready.'

When the crew was gathered around the table, eating as if they hadn't had a square meal since noon, Mack Anderson stepped in, flanked by his foreman. Eating and the small amount of sporadic conversation stopped. Everyone looked at them expectantly. 'Guess you boys prob'ly know by now,' Mack said, 'the Runt busted up the rustlin' ring. He killed three outa the five of 'em, single handed. I sent Les into town a couple days ago to help out, but I guess he missed Runt on the trail. It was over by then anyhow. Runt didn't seem to need any help. He outdrew Joe Tyne an' killed him, too, as one of 'em. So he gets the extra three months' pay I promised. Runt, it's on what I owe you, whenever you draw your time. The rest o' you boys, be on the lookout. Hayhorn's the ringleader o' the bunch, an' he got away. One o' the others did too, and we don't know who that one is. Clint'll likely be showin' up, sooner or later, lookin' to get even, so keep your eyes peeled.'

The rancher turned and left the chow hall, and Frank took his place and began to eat. It seemed to Robert, thinking back later, that he must have answered a hundred questions before the others allowed him to go to bed.

He was scarcely out of bed the next morning when the sound of a running horse brought everybody outdoors. Les Collins rode into the yard on a horse almost run to death. Mack Anderson, wearing pants over long underwear, but no shirt, met him in the yard. 'What's up, Les? You've rode that horse pertneart to death. Frank! Get someone to take care o' this horse, before he drops dead. What's up, Lester?'

'All hell's busted loose in Rock Springs,' Les announced loud enough for all to hear. 'The trouble betwixt the white miners an' the Chinese finally busted out.

The whites, pertneart the whole town an' all the white miners, went an' blocked off the bridges, then went inta Hong Kong an' started killin' ever' Chinaman they could find. Burned down the whole place. Folks looted ever'thing they could find afore it burned up. What Chinese got away lit out barefoot to the south, then likely circled around toward Evanston. They's Chinese at Evanston too, so that's most likely where they went. It was jist like everyone there went plumb loco. I ain't never seen nothin' like it in my life. Even women! Ol' Ma Osborne, what runs the laundry, was even doin' it. She had a shotgun, an' I seen 'er shoot two Chinese with it myself. Then she went an' stole everythin' she could use from the Chinese laundry, then set it on fire.'

Deathly silence settled like a black pall on the ranch yard. Finally someone found his tongue. 'How many did they kill, Les?'

'Musta been upwards of fifty er more.'

'What's goin' on now?'

'The whole town's jist, well, it's like nothin' I ain't never seen. Everyone's jist plumb gone nuts. They's armed mobs a-runnin' around town, tryin' ta loot even the white stores an' such. Ever' store has a bunch o' armed guards tryin' ta keep 'em from it. Folks has lit out ridin' fer the sheriff, an' others ridin' fer the army. Telegraph office is plumb tore down, so they gotta go to Green River ta wire. I jist lit out. Mack, I think we need ta ride the whole crew in there an' help.'

Mack shook his head. 'It'd take us a day to get there, ridin' hard. It took you a day to get here. By the time we get there, the governor'll be there with the army, most likely. Anyway, if he isn't there, all we could do is add one more mob. In a deal like that, nobody knows who's on whose side. We'd just add to the confusion.'

'I gotta go, Mr Anderson.'

All eyes swivelled to Robert. 'I have a girl there,' he said. He could almost hear the tears in his own voice. 'Her father owns the mercantile store. If there's looting, they'll be a target. Army or no army, I have to go.'

'Then go,' Mack said with no hesitation. 'Your job's waitin' when you git back. Mind you, I do use married hands too, if it comes to that. But you watch yourself, ya hear?'

Robert didn't answer. He was already running to the barn. He roped his best horse from those in the corral and saddled quickly. He rode out of the yard fifteen minutes later, riding at a lope. As soon as he could slow the pounding of his heart he reined his horse back to a swift, ground-eating trot. He knew the horse could maintain that pace all day. He mentally calculated the amount of daylight he would have. It was early September. There was plenty of daylight. He should be able to make Rock Springs by dark.

17

Shadows thickened toward dark as Robert came in sight of Rock Springs. Devastation stretched before him. Smoke hung in the air. Ruins of at least sixty hastily built houses smoldered across Bitter Creek. Food, broken porcelain, clothing, furniture, even opium pots littered the streets of what had been dubbed Hong Kong — the Chinese section of Rock Springs. Nothing living moved there.

The streets of the other part of Rock Springs were alive with people. Nobody walked alone. Groups of drunken miners staggered along, singing lustily. Smaller groups of armed miners prowled for anything unguarded they might steal. Honest citizens went in armed groups to do what they had to do, then retreated behind locked and barricaded doors.

Avoiding the business area, Robert

circled to Spaulding's home. It was dark by the time he got there. The house was just as dark. He slipped quietly into the barn behind the residence. He could hear the milk cow chewing her cud, lying in her stall.

He nodded with the assurance the silent bovine provided that nobody else was there. He removed the saddle and bridle from his exhausted horse. He had to force himself to rub the animal down, to fill his water bucket, to fill the manger with hay and the grain box with oats. Every fiber of his being screamed for Sissy, but his training as a cowboy simply wouldn't allow him to put his horse up hot and wet.

As soon as the horse was taken care of, he slipped the rifle from his saddle scabbard. He grabbed an extra box of ammunition for both rifle and pistol from his saddle-bag, and eased out of the barn.

Nothing moved in the yard. No lamp had been lit in the house. Looking about carefully, he ran to the back door, staying as low to the ground as he could. He knocked quietly on the door. 'Anyone there?' he asked. 'It's Robert.'

Nothing stirred. Nobody answered. He listened carefully for several minutes. There was no sound. 'Must be at the store,' he guessed.

Staying to the shadows he hurried to the main street. It was alive with people. Most were drunk and boisterous. The front of every store was boarded over. Raw lumber, hastily nailed over doors and windows, provided only slits for the occupants to see who approached. 'Or to stick a gun through,' Robert surmised.

Moving away from the street he circled around. He approached the back door of Spaulding's Mercantile. Too late he noticed nearly a hundred tin cans, attached to strings, arranged so anyone approaching would trip in the strings and make a great deal of noise. He did.

Dogs began to bark. He distinctly heard the click of three guns being cocked. A voice demanded, 'Who's there?'

He thought the voice was Sissy's father, but he wasn't at all sure. He crouched. He wasn't even aware his gun was in his hand. 'Robert,' he answered softly.

'Robert who?'

'Purdy. Robert Purdy. Are you guys OK?'

Sissy's voice responded. Relief flooded through him. His knees went suddenly weak. 'Is that you, Robert?' she asked.

'Yes. Are you all right?'

'Oh, Robert! Oh, get in here!'

He heard a door open in front of him. He couldn't see at all into the shadows against the building. 'I'm coming,' he said. 'As soon as I can get through this tin can booby trap.'

The sound of Sissy's giggle filled him with delight. He gave up trying to work his way quietly and simply clanked and banged his way to the door. As he stepped through somebody swiftly shut and bolted it. Then Sissy was in his arms.

The whole world with all its troubles retreated to some far away, irrelevant corner of the universe. Everything Robert cared about was in his arms, finding his lips, filling his heart. Only with great effort of will did they finally separate.

'Oh, Robert! I'm so glad to see you! How did you get here so quickly?'

Robert took a deep breath. Norman Spaulding shook his hand. Henrietta, Sissy's mother spoke. 'Are the windows all covered? I'd like to light a lamp.'

A voice Robert didn't recognize said, 'They're covered. Go ahead.'

A match flared. Its glow revealed a kerosene lamp. A disembodied hand removed the chimney and touched the match to the lamp's wick. The light grew. The chimney was replaced. The light diffused and illuminated the room dimly.

The light allowed Robert and Sissy to see each other. They both drank the sight in thirstily. 'How did you get here so quickly?' Sissy repeated.

'Rode my horse half to death! Mr Anderson sent Les Collins down from the ranch to help me out if I found the rustlers,' he explained. 'He got here after it was all over, but then everything busted loose. He rode back to tell Mr Anderson what happened. I just had to come. I couldn't stand the thought of you here without being here to protect you.'

'Oh, Robert! It's been so awful! I haven't seen anything, but the ones we've talked to say they've completely destroyed Hong Kong.'

'It's gone,' he confirmed. 'Looks like … I don't know what it looks like. I've never seen anything like it. Nothing's left, but ashes and burned buildings. Stuff is strung all over the streets. It doesn't look like a place anyone could ever live in.'

'It all happened pretty fast,' Norman observed.

'What caused it? There were hard feelings toward the Chinese when I was working in the mine, but nothing that would cause men to do that.'

'It started out as a fight in Number One Mine,' Norman explained. 'A couple miners named Whitehouse and Jenkins were assigned a room to work. Then they took it away from them and gave it to some Chinese. That started a fight between those two and three or four Chinese. Then everybody else in the mine started getting in on it, the whites

193

against the Chinese. They finally broke it up, but they shut down the mine for the day. Three men were dead. The word got around to all the mines by the next day. The white men in the other mines all stopped working too, and started congregating in town. Then, of course, they all started drinking. They closed down all the saloons at noon, but it was too late. Somebody started a cry to go get rid of all the Chinese, and that started it.'

'All miners?'

'At the beginning, I guess. But it didn't take long for railroad workers to join in. Then, of course, the drifters that happened to be around weren't going to pass up the chance to get in on a chance to run wild.'

The voice Robert hadn't recognized chimed in. He remembered it suddenly as the voice of Ike Woods, the deputy sheriff. 'By the time the mob got to the bridges, they had a plan figured out. They blocked off the bridges so the Chinese couldn't escape, then just started shooting every Chinese they could see. They spread out all through Hong Kong, going after anyone they could find. Some of 'em they robbed an' let go. Most of 'em they just shot, er clubbed with picks. The only way out for the Chinese was straight out south, so they just lit out, runnin' fer their lives. Most of 'em didn't even have shoes on er nothin'.'

'Where did they go?'

'Evanston, mostly. The railroad sent out a train yesterday an' picked up the ones that was left, an' took 'em over there.'

'That were left? You mean the mobs kept chasing them?'

He shook his head. 'No, I don't know that anybody chased 'em much. But a bunch of 'em was shot, an' died out there. It's been plumb cold fer September, too. Some of 'em couldn't take the cold. Wolves got some of 'em, I guess.'

In the circle of his arms Robert felt Sissy shudder. He squeezed her and she pushed harder against him. 'What are you doing about it?' Robert demanded.

The deputy glared at him in the dim

light. 'Tryin' my dangdest to stay alive,' he retorted. 'There ain't nothin' on God's green earth one man kin do out there right now.'

'Have you sent for help?'

Woods nodded. 'We sent for help. I got word to Green River. The sheriff got word to the territorial governor, Francis Warren. He sent for the army, but the army said they couldn't help without the president's orders. So they wired the president, but Cleveland was on vacation somewheres. Nobody in Washington seemed much interested. They're supposed to have the army here in a couple days. The governor's walkin' around town every day to try to show the mobs he ain't afraid of 'em, but he holes up in his railroad car with his guards at night, same's we do.'

Robert sifted the information for several minutes in silence. Finally he said, 'So there's nothing to do but wait, huh?'

'Wait and try to protect what's ours,' Norman agreed. 'We're forted up pretty good here, unless they decide to burn us out. That's not likely. The only reason they'd attack us would be for the guns and provisions and things we have. If they burned us out, they wouldn't be able to get those things anyway. We just moved enough of our things from the house to just stay here. I slip home twice a day to milk the cow and take care of things, then come back.'

'I noticed she'd been milked,' Robert commented.

'Did you put your horse in the barn?' Sissy asked.

Before he could answer, a clatter of cans erupted from outside the back door. It was followed by a volley of profanity. Henrietta quickly blew out the lamp. The darkness was overwhelming.

Norman moved silently to a back window. Pulling aside a blanket that covered the window, he peered outside. 'Whoever it was, he's leaving,' he said. 'The noise scared him off.'

Robert holstered the gun he had realized he had drawn.

He and Sissy eventually found a corner

somewhat away from the others. They went to sleep there, his arm around her as she snuggled against him. He tried to stay awake, just for the sheer delight of feeling her presence. His exhaustion overcame him anyway, and he slept.

At the first streaks of dawn, Norman peered between the boards sheltering the front of his store. 'Street looks pretty quiet,' he announced. 'I guess I better go home and milk.'

'I'll do it,' Robert volunteered.

'I'll go with you,' Sissy said instantly.

Norman frowned. Then he shrugged. 'Should be safe enough. Most of the mob'll be too hungover to do anything before noon.'

'I have to take care of my horse anyway,' Robert added, as if he needed to bolster the case for being the one to go. Especially since Sissy offered to go with him, he couldn't have been forced to stay in the store.

They looked carefully through the back window before unbarring the door.

Nothing seemed out of order. He looked with admiration at the arrangement of cans that made such an effective alarm system. He could see no way to approach the store from the rear without encountering them.

Noticing where he was looking, Sissy explained. 'In daylight, if you're careful, there's just room enough to step between the rows of cans, so you don't wake up the whole neighborhood.'

'I made enough noise last night, I doubt they're sleeping yet anyway,' he observed.

She giggled as they made their way out the door, through the maze of cans, and along the street. At the barn Sissy volunteered to milk the cow, while Robert carried water, forked hay, and measured out grain for the cow and his horse. They finished quickly and were just ready to leave when Sissy stopped abruptly.

Robert bumped into her, and grabbed her to keep her from falling. 'What did you stop for?'

Silently she pointed. Just inside the

front door of the small barn were two sets of saddle-bags. She turned to face him and mouthed silently, 'Are those yours?'

He shook his head. His eyes darted around the barn. There was no place in the barn anyone could have been sleeping or hiding without his noticing them. He had been in the hay mow, the grain bin and the tack room while tending the animals.

'Whoever they belong to, they aren't here,' he assured her. 'Let's see what's in them.'

Looking around carefully, they walked to the saddle-bags. As he tipped them up so he could open one, he grunted. 'Wow! Heavy!'

He opened the flap. It was almost half full of gold coins. He quickly confirmed that all four bags were about equally filled. He whistled softly. 'That is a lot of money!' he said.

'Whose could it be?' Sissy marveled. She walked out in front of the barn, looking around again. 'Who would leave that much money just sitting there?'

As if in answer, two horses came around the corner of the barn. The riders stopped abruptly when they saw Robert and Sissy.

'Well, whatd'ya know?' Clint Hayhorn found his voice first. 'Look at what we got here!'

Both Clint and his companion stepped off their horses and stepped away from them. Both held their hands within inches of their guns. Hayhorn was less than three feet from Sissy. The other man was about six feet to Hayhorn's right. Both men faced Robert.

Clint grinned. 'Lew, meet The Runt. This here's that greenhorn runt I was tellin' you about. He's also the one what busted up our operation and killed the rest o' the boys.'

Lew's eyes never blinked. He stared at Robert with a cold, flat gaze. Clint continued. 'Runt, meet Lew Potter. I hear you went an' outdrew Joe Tyne. Well I got news for you. Lew here's so fast he allays made Joe look like an amateur. I guess you know what that means.'

'Where'd all the money come from?' Robert demanded.

Clint's grin widened. 'Us to know, you to wonder,' he taunted. 'It's all ours, though. More money'n you'll ever see. I'll say one thing for you, though, Runt. You got good taste in women. Me'n Lew'll enjoy yore woman a whole bunch soon's we git rid o' you.'

Sissy gasped. As if it was a signal, both men grabbed for their guns.

Robert's gun seemed to fly into his hand of its own accord. Lew's gun was just lifting from his holster when Robert's gun barked. The gunman grunted and continued lifting the barrel of his gun. The shot he fired kicked dirt at Robert's feet. Robert's second shot drove him back a step. He faltered, then tried again to raise the gun. The third shot from Robert's gun broke the effort and he collapsed. Robert whirled the gun to cover Clint.

Clint was still smiling. He had moved directly behind Sissy. His arm wrapped around her shoulders, holding her tightly against him. His gun covered Robert.

Robert knew he dared not shoot.

'Purty fast, Runt,' Clint conceded. 'You just doubled my share o' the money. Now drop the gun, er I kill you an' yore woman both.'

Robert's mind cast about desperately. A sudden thought struck him. He grinned. The smile had the desired effect. It caused Clint to hesitate. 'What're you grinnin' about?'

Robert spoke. He spoke to Clint, but his gaze was into Sissy's eyes. 'Oh, I was just remembering something. You look exactly like someone I used to know.'

'I do?'

'Yes, you do. Dead ringer, as a matter of fact. His name was Rick Donavan.'

He stressed the name as he said it. Understanding lit a spark in Sissy's eyes. She carefully lifted a booted foot. Then she stomped down as hard as she could on Clint's toe.

Clint let out an involuntary howl. His grip relaxed for just an instant. Sissy relaxed just as quickly, dropping straight down out of his grip.

She was only half way to the ground when Robert's gun barked twice. The shots were so close together they sounded like one elongated shot.

Clint's gun barked as well. Splinters flew from the edge of the barn door. He tried to swear. All he could manage was to open his mouth. He took a step backward. He fell backward, sprawled full length on the ground. He didn't move.

Sissy scrambled from the ground and ran to Robert. 'Oh, Robert! Oh, I was so scared! Oh, darling! Are you all right? Did you get hit?'

'I'm fine,' Robert assured her. 'I was scared too, let me tell you!'

She stayed there in his arms until she stopped trembling. It took a while. Then she pulled away from him. 'All that money! What will happen to it?'

He shrugged. 'We'll have to take it to Ike. If there's a record of it being stolen from someone, which I'm sure it is, then they'll get it back. But if there isn't, I guess it'll be ours.'

'Then we could start our own ranch?'

He pondered the thought for a long moment. 'Then we could start our own ranch.'

'Oh, darling. That's just too much. From the most terrifying time of my life to the answer to all our dreams, all in just minutes!'

'Life is like that sometimes,' he observed. 'I was sure hoping you'd remember that story about Donavan, and know what I wanted you to do.'

'Oh, darling, you knew I'd remember. I have never forgotten a single thing you've ever said to me. And I never will.'

She would, of course. But it seemed to summarize her feelings at the moment, so she just let it stand.

We do hope that you have enjoyed reading this large print book.

Did you know that all of our titles are available for purchase?

We publish a wide range of high quality large print books including:
Romances, Mysteries, Classics
General Fiction
Non Fiction and Westerns

Special interest titles available in large print are:
The Little Oxford Dictionary
Music Book, Song Book
Hymn Book, Service Book

Also available from us courtesy of Oxford University Press:
Young Readers' Dictionary
(large print edition)
Young Readers' Thesaurus
(large print edition)

For further information or a free brochure, please contact us at:
Ulverscroft Large Print Books Ltd.,
The Green, Bradgate Road, Anstey,
Leicester, LE7 7FU, England.
Tel: (00 44) **0116 236 4325**
Fax: (00 44) **0116 234 0205**

Other titles in the
Linford Western Library:

THE BROKEN TRAIL

Alexander Frew

After a gang of robbers tries to kill him on the trail to Coker, Cody is lost and wounded. When he finally arrives in town, the corrupt sheriff blames him for the murder of a prominent citizen, who was slain by the same gang. Cody vows that he will unleash death and destruction on the men who embroiled him in this fight — but he has been thrown into a tiny cell, falsely identified by the widow of the dead man, and today, without trial, he must hang . . .

DEAD MAN RIVER

Tyler Hatch

At first, it seemed to Dave Brent like a wonderful solution to his troubles: exchange identities with the dead man he found floating in the river, and that should be the last he'd hear of the Vandemanns, who wanted his blood. But the dead man was more popular than Dave reckoned — and a lot of men want to find the one now using his name. If they catch him, they intend to offer him a choice of deaths — by torture or a quick bullet. Dave isn't keen on either option . . .

BAD NIGHT AT
THE CRAZY BULL

John Dyson

After a night of drinking at the
Crazy Bull Hotel, Glen Stone wakes
up to find himself in bed with a
saloon girl who informs him that
they have been married. When Glen
returns with her to his ranch, he
must deal with her refusal to do her
share of the work, the assorted
unsavoury characters her presence
attracts, and the wrath of his long-
time intended and her father. Will
the arrival of horse preacher Repen-
tance Rathbone restore harmony to
the lives of the Wyoming ranchers?

CHILCOT'S REDEMPTION

Ethan Harker

Brook Chilcot's career as a sheriff ended after a disastrous shootout, and he is in no hurry to forgo his alcoholic haze. But when a young man wishing to be taught how to shoot convinces him to leave retirement, Brook returns to the town of Grafton's Peak, where he must deal with new faces and old enemies. As the son of an outlaw he killed many years ago arrives to confront him, Chilcot is given the chance to make up for his errors in the past. Will he take it?